FLIRTING WITH FIRE

A Noble Pass Affaire Novella

Enjoy the heat!

Misty Dietz

A Noble Pass Affaire Novella Series

Flirting with Fire by Misty Dietz

Flirting with Disaster by Josie Matthews

Flirting with Sin by Naima Simone

Flirting with Fate by Jerrie Alexander

Flirting with the Devil by Kym Roberts

Other Titles by Misty Dietz

Come Hell or High Desire

A Noble Pass Affaire Novella

FLIRTING with Fire

MISTY DIETZ

Misty Media

FLIRTING WITH FIRE

Misty Media
SEPTEMBER 2015
eBook ISBN: 978-1-943716-00-5
Print ISBN: 978-1-943716-01-2

Cover illustrator: Misty Dietz,
www.MistyDietz.com
Edited by: Pam Dougherty,
www.TheWriteActor.com
Interior design by: Top-ePublishing Services,
www.Top-ePublishingServices.com

This book is a work of fiction. Names, characters, places, and incidents are the product of the author's imagination or are used fictitiously. Any resemblance to actual persons, living or dead, business establishments, events, or locales is entirely coincidental.

Special Thanks

This book was so much fun to write, mostly because this series was a joint project with four other Chick Swagger ladies: Kym, Jerrie, Josie, and Naima – thanks for all the brainstorming, laughs, and hand holding on my first self-publishing journey! Thanks also to Denise, Heather, and Jo, critiquers-extraordinaire; to Deb and Robin, my favorite beta readers; to the sassy and all-around wonderful ladies of the Chick Swagger Sirens, who are my daily dose of irreverence; and last but not least, to my family for always supporting my dreams, even when leftovers are on the menu…again.

Love and hugs to you all!

*To my David, the best suite mate a girl
could ever have*

One

September

Ivy Bradford peered out the car window, trying to appreciate the mist-shrouded mountains while her two best friends argued over which of their boyfriends was the better lover.

Monique took one hand off the wheel and ran a palm against her intricate cornrows with a captivating smile. "Speaking of sex, you gotta text us a picture of your suite mate as soon as it's not creepy to take one. If he's half as attractive as my man, you guys may spend more time in your room than in the great outdoors. He passed his background check, right?"

Ah yes, the *suite mate*.

Ivy had noticed that not-so-minor detail just last night in the fine print of the contest

1

coordinator's email. Two months ago when Monique and Kay had recorded her video entry for the resort's monthly contest, Ivy hadn't anticipated sharing quarters with *anyone* if she won.

Well, she'd won. And this suite mate thing was troubling.

She waved a hand in the air, striving for nonchalance. "What makes you think my suite mate will be male?"

Monique snickered. "What makes you think he won't be? Come on, Ivy, a contest called *A Noble Pass Affaire* that asks for your sexual preference on the entry form? You're an intelligent woman. Put two and two together."

For the third time in the two hour jaunt from Grand Junction to Noble Pass, Colorado, Ivy wished she'd driven alone. *You don't need wheels at that snazzy place,* they'd said. *We entered you in the contest so it's our responsibility to get you there and then pick you up at the end of the week.*

She'd foolishly conceded. "It's advertised as a week of rest and relaxation, not some x-rated rendezvous, Monique." Her belly was fluttering like it was, though, dammit.

Of course she'd heard the rumors that Castle Alainn's new monthly contest was more like a blind date than the you-deserve-a-break sweepstakes it was being promoted as. But Ivy had her own reasons for accepting a week at the fabulous mountain retreat. "It'll be a great location to film an adventure documentary for the kids." And hopefully overcome her fear of heights, since her fourth graders had appointed themselves her champions to overcome the phobia.

Monique slid Ivy one of those are-you-kiddin'-me looks. "Your head's in the sand, girl. You know about the resort's match-making owners. Every TV station in Colorado has run their story."

Well, duh. Their names were Liam and Alana Fitzgerald. Ivy had tuned into their epic love story every time it ran on a different channel. She'd even recorded it. "Elderly, eccentric, and besotted. Just because they own a castle doesn't mean they're foisting their romantic ideals on everyone else."

"I agree with Monique on this one," Kay said from the backseat. "Not only does *A Noble Pass Affaire* play up a sexual theme, Colorado's naughtiest radio station sponsored the contest. I wonder how they'll structure the week. Will it be like Hedonism in Jamaica, or—"

"*Stop.*" Ivy twisted in her seat to peer at her oldest friend. Kay's striking green eyes blinked calmly behind her vintage-fifties tortoiseshell glasses. Ivy tried not to grin because that would only incite more of Kay's sexual speculation—something she was exceedingly good at. "I highly doubt they'll allow topless volleyball and orgies on the docks."

Kay absently pushed her long blonde hair over her shoulder. "Nevertheless, did you bring protection?"

"Great conversation for a bunch of elementary school teachers," Ivy murmured.

"Don't be a prude," Kay scolded, in that sexy, condescending librarian tone that made all the male teachers in their school district a little stupid.

"I've got a bunch if you don't." Monique leaned over Ivy's lap to pop the glove box.

Ivy shook her head, unable to hold back the smile any longer. "Gee, how could I ever survive without you guys?"

Monique's big laugh filled the car, then suspiciously quieted. "You know I love you,

4

right?"

Uh oh. That was Monique's not-so-subtle way of starting a serious discussion "Not now, okay? I want things—"

"*Sparkly.* Yeah, we know." Kay pushed at the bridge of her glasses in a way that should be *so* nerdy, but God, it just wasn't. "But you can't fool us, Ivy. You want people laughing instead of fighting, and you have enough charm to make a continent damn near reshape itself. But here's the thing...people from all over the world vacation at Castle Alainn. The likelihood of knowing someone there is extremely minimal, so be yourself without that breezy, socialite superficiality you wear like armor. You're good enough as you are."

Ivy breathed deep to calm her revving heart rate. "I thought you guys were being sweet to enter me in the contest and then drive me here, but instead it's looking like some kind of intervention. Why don't you pull over so I can be suitably cowed."

"Don't be so dramatic," Monique grumbled. "Kay nailed it. No matter what's going on in your life, you act like it's all rainbows and unicorns. Like when your parents missed your Colorado Teacher of the Year banquet. You're always there for their fancy-pants galas and tributes, but the one time you wanted them to be there for *you*, they couldn't make it. You acted like it was no big deal, yet you *had* to have been disappointed."

Crushed was more like it.

Only she knew her parents' absence wasn't because of an emergency. Rather, they had *forgotten*.

"And what about that smarmy substitute teacher who took all the credit in the media for *your* students' chocolate milk protest?" Kay asked.

Monique banged on the steering wheel. "Yeah! You're the one who did all the planning, organizing, and banner-making with the kids. The sub just happened to be the one who showed up on the day you were sick. Pisses me off that she accepted what should have been *your* limelight! And it irritates me that you blew it off. It's okay to get mad sometimes, you know."

No, it's not.

Never let them see you sweat, Ivy. That had been the mandate from her economics professor father before her first piano recital. She was eight. He'd apparently been so pleased with his advice that it became his primary message to her for nearly two decades.

"The focus should have been on the kids, not any adults. It was their voice that needed to be heard," Ivy said.

Kay sighed. "The point is, frustration without a release valve isn't healthy."

Ivy compressed her lips. "So much for starting the week off on a high note. Maybe my documentary will be *How* not *to start a vacation.* Or better yet, *How to dump intrusive friends before you're in too deep.*"

"Sometimes I wonder if your students are the only ones who see your authentic self. Stop the *everything-is-perfect-all-the-time* show, Ivy. Let down your guard for the rest of us."

Kay was annoyed, but so what? She was the one who'd started this fast moving train to can-of-wormsville. Ivy looked down at her hands. "If you give people anything other than charming, you're gambling with disaster. Look at my parents."

Ack. She'd said too much. Now these two would pick and pry until her ears bled. The truth was, people wanted roses without the thorns. Her parents had drilled that into her head with the same ferocity as her private tutors had schooled her in quantum physics and statistics.

"Your parents are cool, right?" Monique's concerned glance made Ivy's chest tighten.

"Sure, if your idea of 'cool' is fifty shades of phony."

"They love you," Kay protested.

"Not as much as their careers. Maybe not even as much as the library named in their honor." Ivy's laughter came easy after years of practice packing mud over her feelings. Stuffing them down under ever-hardening layers that looked organized and perfect from the outside. She was her parents' beloved trophy child— witty and engaging on cue for her father's esteemed academic associates and her mother's Ivy League medical colleagues.

And their deepest disappointment when she dared reveal anything less than a cultivated, pleasant facade.

Kay put her hand on Ivy's shoulder. "It's okay to be sad sometimes."

"And lonely." Monique pulled into Castle Alainn's parking lot.

"Are you two done? My life is good. I have the best job, two nosy, but good-hearted friends—"

"And an arid sex life." Monique's full lips curved as she turned off the car.

"Oh come on, it hasn't been *that* long," Ivy insisted.

Monique raised an eyebrow. "You haven't had anyone in your bed since jackass Joey, and he was what, six months ago?"

"Bam! There's another good example of Ivy writing off a shit-situation with smiles and aw-shucks shrugs," Kay said, then high-fived Monique.

Ivy wrinkled her nose in memory of the Joey-debacle. Unfortunately, some douche bags were good in the sack and convincing apologists. Her bullshit radar had let her down big time in his case. "*Whatever,* you guys. Dissect me all the way back to Grand Junction, if you like. I'm going to check into paradise now." She put her fingers on the door handle.

Kay hurriedly exited the car and opened Ivy's door. "We worry about you. It's not normal to be so happy all the time."

"Do you realize how ridiculous that sounds?" Ivy unbuckled her seatbelt, wishing she could rewind the morning and say goodbye to these two in Grand Junction instead of here. "Maybe I ought to stop slumming with my fourth graders and start my own Rainbows and Unicorns Self-Help Empire. People pay good money for that kind of thing, you know."

When Monique and Kay traded glances, it felt like her parents passing judgment all over again. Well, screw that. She was moments from checking in at this magnificent resort, and she was *not* going to let these two stress her out.

The sprawling castle butted up against Lake Noble's rocky cliffs, the roof sporting dozens of Gothic peaks, the sides textured and multi-hued in earthen colors. Ivy breathed in the crisp, alpine air, hoping to ease the constricting in her chest as she gazed at those scary high cliffs.

I can do this.

First, though, she had to get rid of these humbugs. "Would you please be happy that I'm happy?"

Kay's eyes bored into her. "Deep down you're hurting, Ivy."

"*Mmm hmm*, growing up with an absentee mommy and daddy leaves wounds," Monique added.

"*Wounds?* Lighten up with the psycho

babble and give me a hug before I unfriend you both."

Monique and Kay exchanged one more of those irritating, do-you-think-she's-really-okay looks before moving toward her. Kay wrapped her arms around Ivy's neck. "You don't need to be 'on' all the time to make the world love you."

When Kay stepped away, Monique's arms came around Ivy like a straight jacket. "What Kay said; you don't need to put on an act, sugar."

Ivy pressed a kiss on Monique's satiny, cocoa cheek, then disengaged. "You guys are sweet, but there's no act." She pulled up the handle on her rolling suitcase, fighting the urge to sprint inside so she didn't have to listen to any more of their lectures. Regardless of what they thought, everything was fine.

At least until her parents returned from mom's much-hyped Doctors Without Borders trip. Then she'd have to explain why she'd indulged in a frivolous vacation when she could have been doing something to elevate the family name in the community.

Ugh.

You have seven, guilt-free days. Make the

most of them.

That's what she'd told herself last night as she'd packed. This weekend had three purposes really. Film an adventure documentary, ease her fear of heights, and learn how to let go of her guilt over disappointing her parents.

Fake it till you make it.

Ivy smiled wider at Kay and Monique. "If it makes you feel better, I'll text pictures of the mountains, my fine dining, and of course, all my activities, so you can see how depressed and wounded I am."

Monique's whole body deflated. "Aww, now don't be like that."

Kay's face had that you're-disappointing-me look that made Ivy feel like a toddler who'd yanked all the hair off her doll's head.

"If you feel unsafe or uncomfortable with your suite mate—even for a moment—trust your gut and demand a separate room. It's your right per the contest guidelines. Or better yet, call us. We'll come get you." Kay got into the car. "I stand by my assertion, Ivy. Be open. *For once.*"

When Kay closed the door and started the engine from the passenger side, Monique looked at Ivy with puppy dog eyes like she didn't know whether to stay or go.

That damn Kay. She always had to have the last word.

She was almost always right, too.

"Well, bye then," Ivy breathed after Monique got into the car with a half-hearted wave.

In moments, her friends were gone. Ivy turned to face the castle, burying pinpricks of disquiet under deliberate layers of anticipation until the unease was no more.

This week was long overdue. And it would be amazing.

If only by sheer force of will.

Two

"What do you mean, *suite mate*? I was under the impression I won seven days of solitude, not a week of bunking with a total stranger." Cole Castillo turned on his younger sister who'd entered him in this crazy contest without his knowledge. "Did you know this from the start, Mya?"

"Please keep your voice down, Mr. Castillo." Castle Alainn's on-duty assistant manager—his polished name badge said CONWAY—quickly closed the door to the elegant, wood paneled office. "Our contest is certainly no gauche hook up." Conway directed Cole to sit in one of the expensive-looking leather chairs like he was one of their regular posh guests instead of a run-of-the-mill fireman.

Maybe Mya had padded his contest entry more than she'd let on.

14

Then it dawned on him.

He shot out of the chair. "You. Little. *Brat*. This is a blind date?"

Mya shrugged and grinned with the dimples that had saved her butt for two decades. "I didn't know for sure, but there was gossip. Come on, Cole, it'll be fun. Your year from hell is turning you into a fuddy-duddy. Even your boss thinks you need some time off."

Mierda. Cole should have known something was up as soon as he'd tried to check in and the front desk staff had whisked him in here, all stifled giggles and sly looks. He marched to the door. "I'm done here. If you're not in my truck in five minutes, you can hitchhike back to Fort Collins, Mya." He had too many responsibilities at home to waste time indulging in frat boy misadventures. That ship had sailed when his father was gunned down on a domestic abuse call ten years ago.

Mya ran ahead of him, placing herself as blockade against the door. Cole would have laughed at her puny deterrence if he hadn't been so dog-tired.

"At least meet her!" she cried.

He glared at his sister. "I don't have to do

anything. This was over the top, even for you."

"*Lo siento.* Don't be mad. All you've ever done is take care of our *familia*. I want you to have some carefree memories tucked in with all the serious, responsible ones. Please meet her. The owners have supposedly matched you two out of five hundred entries."

"Seven hundred eighty-eight entries," Conway corrected. "And she happens to be from Colorado. That was amazing odds considering the entries came from all over the United States."

"Oh wow, see? Cole, *pleeease.*"

This whole thing was ridiculous. "Move away from the door, Mya."

She gathered her long, black hair into one fist like she always did when she'd decided to dig in her heels. Then she smiled sweetly at the assistant manager. "Can I have a minute alone with my brother?"

When Conway quietly left the room, Mya re-closed the door.

Cole sighed. "I'm not doing this, *lobito.*"

"Buttering me up with the *little wolf* bit won't work this time. If you don't meet this woman, I'll tell the fire chief you're getting

16

worse."

Anger flared through his gut at her underhanded tactics, quickly followed by pain and relentless guilt. Mya knew what had happened the day the station responded to a call from a girl trapped by flames in her bedroom. He'd been the one to encourage his sister to apply for the job in the Administrative Services Division of the Poudre Fire Authority, the entity that protected the city of Fort Collins and two-hundred-thirty-five miles of the surrounding area.

Bad call, Castillo. "Your meddling has limits, and you're way over the line here."

"It's not just me, Cole. Since Stan's death, the whole firehouse has watched you. The chief will put you on administrative duty and send you to grief counseling if he continues to hear reports that, contrary to your claims, you're not bouncing back."

Cole's chest ached with memories of falling through the burning floor and hearing his buddy's agonized voice over their helmet radios. Why did it always feel like hours instead of months since that tragic day? "Why would you do something like this...after everything?"

Mya's eyes hardened. "I'm not letting you

retreat into that dark place anymore. It's time to stop hiding and start living. Tough love hurts, Cole. You taught us that."

He stared her down, but she didn't flinch. The moments ticked by as laughter rang out in the lobby. All too soon the space around them became quiet once more. Still, she didn't look away or make this about herself.

She's finally growing up. The realization made him both sad and relieved.

He'd meet this other winner to get Mya off his back. Then when his sister saw for her stubborn-self how absurd this contest was, he'd be in the clear to get the hell outta Dodge. When he got home, he'd offer to help his neighbor fix a leaky roof. He'd also heard that the goodwill store needed strong backs for delivering furniture to the homeless shelter, and God knew Stan's wife needed all kinds of assistance. "Fine, let's get this over with."

Mya threw herself in his arms. "This is going to be fabulous!" She opened the door and Conway stumbled inside, his face turning an unbelievable shade of red when he met Cole's frown.

The assistant manager cleared his throat, straightened his bow tie, and gestured for them to follow. The castle was nearly as stunning as the landscape on which it perched. Slabs of limestone on the staircase gave way to intimate hallways of luxurious hardwoods and tall windows that accommodated breathtaking views of crystalline Lake Noble.

Conway led them to the end of the second floor where autumn sunshine spilled upon a paneled door. A muted voice coming from inside that room made Cole's pulse pound at the base of his throat.

As Conway opened the door, Mya clapped in anticipation, the little shit. His sister's excitement did nothing to soothe his sudden anxiety. Meeting someone new and having to pretend like he was something or someone he wasn't...

This can't work.

Conway opened his arm expansively like Cole was stepping onto a red carpet or something equally pretentious. "This way please."

The main living area held matching white leather chairs, a luxurious sofa, and a two-sided fireplace in one of the bedroom walls. Cole wandered to the wall of windows, mesmerized by the spectacular view of the Rockies when

19

Mya grabbed his arm and, with a giggle, steered him to the second bedroom where he saw...

A blur of bare feet, tan legs, a mouthwatering ass in khaki shorts, and gold-streaked brown hair set to flying as a woman jumped—*jumped*—on the king-sized bed facing an enormous oil painting over the headboard, her back to them.

A smile tugged Cole's mouth, but he flattened his lips when Mya sent him a look of triumph. His social anxiety returned ten-fold.

Conway edged around to the woman's field of vision and waved hesitantly. The woman gasped and spun to face them as she tore her ear buds out with one hand and clasped a micro video camera to her chest with the other. In the blink of an eye, she recovered from her surprise, plopped to her butt, a pretty blush on her cheeks and a blinding smile that nearly stopped Cole's heart.

"Hi." She turned off her music, set the tiniest video camera he'd ever seen on the bed, and stood to approach them. She reached for Mya's hand first. "I'm Ivy."

Mya shifted to smirk at Cole's bemused expression before he could wipe it into oblivion—*hijo de puta*—then she moved into

Ivy's personal space to haul her in for a death-grip hug.

He recognized that look. Mya understood him better than his other two siblings. That look meant *she knew* he'd felt a jolt when he saw Ivy. A jolt that wasn't anything like the pain he'd cocooned around himself these last many months.

A fluttery, messy something like...interest.

Cole scrubbed a hand down the side of his face when he couldn't resist another glance at Ivy's plush lips, blue eyes, and tangled hair. There was something undeniably compelling about her.

It can come to nothing.

He quelled a flare of disappointment, steeling himself to wish Ivy a good week.

Alone.

Hopefully Mya's anger would manifest into silent-treatment on the way home because he craved quiet. He didn't need her raging at him, telling him he was making an epic mistake.

The mistake would be staying.

No way in hell could he atone for his sins with a roommate like Ivy.

Three

Ivy froze when the dainty woman's arms came around her with the strength of a village-terrorizing boa constrictor. From the level of excitement radiating from the gorgeous Latina, she *had* to be her suite mate. The first chance she got, she was texting Monique an I-told-you-so.

The last of Ivy's anxiety evaporated as the woman's infectious laughter triggered her own, and she returned the surprising affection until the petite, dark-haired tornado pulled away to clap her hands with squawks of happiness. Ivy tried not to stare at the arresting man frowning by her bedroom door. The man was tall with coal-black hair and olive-skin, all Bronte-brooding and not quite civilized.

And frankly, impossible to ignore.

Some people just had that sort of presence. This guy possessed tsunami-level waves of it.

Ivy tore her gaze away from the man's intense scrutiny to smile at the woman. "You haven't told me your name!"

"Sorry! I'm Mya Castillo." Her quick, intimate look at the man by the door made Ivy's heart squeeze with a flare of longing. These two obviously shared a communication frequency forged over time.

Husband? Ivy didn't see a wedding ring on either of them. *Must be her boyfriend.* "Nice to meet you, Mya. I hope you aren't camera shy." Ivy held up her mini video camera. "I'll be documenting the week for my fourth graders. It started with my oh-so-cultured bed jumping. I hope to get more sophisticated by tomorrow when I hit the trails."

"Oh my God, you're perfect for each other!" Mya bounced up and down as her boyfriend clenched his teeth and the assistant manager looked like the cat that ate the canary.

Ivy tried to keep her smile in place, but her cheeks wobbled. "What?"

"Oh *chica*, as much as I would love to spend

the week with you, your suite mate winner is *mi hermano*, Cole."

Brother?

Mya's continued chatter melted into white noise in the background as Mr. Dark and Dangerous raised gorgeous hazel eyes to hers. Intelligence, pain, and all-out *warning* projected from his gaze.

Good grief, he totally didn't want to be here.

She could see his and Mya's resemblance now. The insider looks they shared made sense, too, though as an only child, Ivy could only dream about that kind of connection.

Cole turned to Conway. "Mya will have my week."

"Oh, no, you don't!" Mya chased after his broad back.

Conway folded his hands calmly in front of his perfectly fitted sport coat. "Castle Alainn owners Mr. and Mrs. Fitzgerald choose the monthly winners based on the submitted video essays and biographies. I understand that your sister entered you without your full understanding of the contest subtleties, Mr. Castillo, but either you stay as the authentic prize winner, or unfortunately, everyone—

including Ms. Bradford—will have to return home post haste."

Cole sent a look to Mya that promised reckoning.

Mya beamed back.

Oh Jesus, his sister had tricked him.

Fix the discord. Ivy's gaze fell upon a brochure for the Oktoberfest events going on in the resort village this week. She took a deep breath, then smiled at Cole, hoping the quivering edges of her lips weren't too noticeable. "I was really looking forward to this week, so I'll make you a deal." She walked to the antique secretary, picked up the brochure, and pointed to the cover. "I bet I can beat you at the brat eating contest. It starts..." she opened to the schedule, "in forty minutes. If I win, you stay and help me document a week of outdoor adventures for my fourth graders. If you win, I will pack up my things and move to a different room at my own expense." She stuck her hand out. "Deal?"

"That's not a fair contest!" Mya exclaimed.

As Cole approached, the sudden amused warmth in his brownish-gold and green eyes made Ivy's throat dry up. He placed a large, rough palm against hers, his fingers firm and assertive. "Deal."

His sister jerked up her hands with an exaggerated sigh. *"Me cago en todo lo que se menea!"*

"Enough drama, Mya. I see no reason to shit on anything." Cole's deep, slightly accented voice slid against Ivy's skin, so different from any other tone she'd ever heard. Resonant, like a full symphony orchestra, yet also curiously restrained.

She rubbed her arms, tearing her gaze from Cole's ridiculous eyelashes to the resort employee when he bowed.

"Very good. Shall I send for your bags, Mr. Castillo?" Conway asked.

"No need," Cole said. "After I win the contest, I'll be on the road in less than an hour. If you have a blanket for sale, however, my sister might appreciate the warmth as she'll be sitting in the bed of my truck on our way home."

Ivy slammed her bedroom door a little harder than she'd planned after the Castillos and Conway walked back into the suite's common areas. Seriously, could she have come up with a more repugnant ploy to get him to stay? A bratwurst-eating contest. What guy would find that attractive?

Real feminine, Ivy.

She rolled her eyes and walked to the window, staring at the red, orange, and yellows in the fall foliage at the base of the pine-covered mountains. Who was she kidding? Sure, she'd had lots of practice acting like a girly-girl because that was what her parents wanted.

But being overtly feminine wasn't *her.*

She was a ride-on-the-bicycle-handlebars, get-her-hands-dirty explorer who always wanted to know *what* and *how* and *why.*

Her parents never seemed to get that.

Or if they did, they certainly didn't think it was best for her.

Like her career.

Teaching is a fine occupation, Ivy, but you have a scholarship to Harvard. Why waste it on elementary education? You could be a full professor at an Ivy-League school...you could publish, for heaven's sake!

So she'd followed the path her parents laid out for her because, despite their arrogance, she loved them. But ultimately, she hadn't been able to forsake her love of children. So she'd become a Harvard-trained elementary school teacher.

And her parents would never forgive her for it.

She looked at the doorway where Cole had stood.

She didn't want to go home.

Didn't want to switch rooms either.

Cole had a good six inches on her five foot seven frame, and probably fifty pounds. Sure, she'd been the reigning brat-eating champ in eighth grade, but she'd been bigger than most boys in junior high. *I can do this.* One day and night of feeling like the Goodyear blimp would be worth the rest of the week, right?

Someone knocked loudly right before Mya barged in and slammed the door behind her. She chewed her lip, then nodded thoughtfully. Ivy could keep up with fourth graders' mercurial mood shifts, but this woman's emotional range was in a category all her own.

Ivy ran her fingers through her snarly hair. "You're not real big on boundaries, are you?"

Mya's smile was genuine, but brief. "We don't have time for boundaries. Not if we're going to get this contest to stick." She pointed at Ivy's unopened suitcase on the floor. "You got a gunny sack in there, or something that won't bind your guts too tightly?"

Ivy hoisted her suitcase onto the dresser with an absurd smile. This was foolish and reckless and...

Fun!

While she calculated how many days' worth of sodium and saturated fat she'd be ingesting, Mya grabbed Ivy's ratty black yoga pants, stretched the waistband every which way, then tossed them at her. "These will have to do. When was the last time you ate?" she asked.

Ivy held the pants to her chest, feeling her heart drum against her hand. "Drill sergeant much?"

Mya raised a surly eyebrow.

"Don't worry, I had a bowl of cereal this morning. It's long gone."

Mya's frown melted. "I'm sorry. I want this for Cole so much. He's given up more than you can imagine for our family. It's time for some excitement in his life. You're just what he needs."

Ivy glanced up, then quickly back down before Mya could see how the comment affected her.

She'd *never* been just what *anyone* needed.

Ivy left the bathroom door open a crack while she changed clothes and Mya chattered about her steadfast, 'boring' brother who blamed himself for a fellow fire fighter's death while rescuing a thirteen-year-old girl. Come to find out, Cole not only financially supported and cared for a mother with ALS, but also their two younger siblings who weren't even out of high school yet.

Unreal.

How ironic that she'd finally met a man who seemed mature and interesting on a whole new level, yet here she was, slipping into her shabbiest get up, about to stuff her face full of greasy brats.

Her parents would be mortified.

Her fourth graders would quote *The Lion King* and sing, *hakuna matata, Ms. Ivy.*

Sometimes children knew best.

Four

Cole took his seat at one of the tables, the smell of bratwursts overpowering even the crisp, alpine air. Noble Pass resembled ski resort villages all over the world. Quaint, pedestrian-friendly, and too damn crowded. There had to be three hundred people milling around, laughing and visiting on the grassy area in front of the plaza's stage where the contestants would soon be clogging their arteries.

Cole tried not to glance two bodies to the right where Ivy chatted animatedly with the barrel-chested contestant between them who wore a foam hat in the shape of a bratwurst. This was going to be the easiest bet he'd ever won. Ivy was taller than Mya by a few inches, but she was as lithe and graceful as the willow tree they'd planted in their back yard a decade ago, right after his father's funeral.

31

Ivy moved and swayed like the slim branches, too, so lovely and almost supernaturally supple.

Listen to you. He'd stopped writing poetry years ago. It had been helpful during the dark days after his father's murder, but he'd outgrown such silly scribblings. And he sure as hell didn't want anyone to find out.

Firefighters didn't write poetry.

Or compare interesting women to willow trees.

When someone set a steaming plate of bratwursts before him, he turned to look at Ivy again. There was no way she could fit more brats in that trim belly than he could. *Too bad*, he thought before he reminded himself he had too many responsibilities, too many goals to indulge in frivolous blind dates. Someone like Ivy with her carefree smile and adventurous spirit would tease out the recklessness in his blood that he'd worked so hard to suppress.

Recklessness is why Stan is dead.

Cole pressed chilled fingertips to his eyelids, but knew he didn't deserve the relief of erasing the memory of Stan's wife collapsing when he and Chief Bogart had delivered the horrible news. When Cole opened his eyes, Ivy was watching him, concern and curiosity intermingled on her features.

You okay? she mouthed. Her lips were a lovely shape, soft and a surprisingly dark pink. When those lips curved, his eyes tracked upward. She had the cutest nose he'd ever seen. When his gaze finally rose to her eyes, he found laughter and a frank awareness that made his groin tighten for the first time in a long while.

A lean man in suspenders and a green felt hat tapped on a microphone. After he announced the contest rules, Ivy raised her beer stein, drawing the attention of everyone within a twenty-foot radius. "Cheers to Oktoberfest!"

The brat-headed giant leaned toward Cole. "I've been seeing you two make eyes at each other. You're a lucky bastard to have a girl who does this kinda thing."

Not my girl, he should have replied, but didn't. He didn't care to consider why. He hadn't always been dull. Once upon a time he'd been fearless and brash.

I'm sorry, Stan.

Cole's hands curled into fists in his lap as the announcer cued the contestants to get ready.

He looked at Ivy one last time. Ten minutes and a gut-ache later, he'd be on his way to his truck. He'd never see the intriguing school teacher again. He looked down at the plate of brats, and for a moment, considered letting her win.

But unfortunately, rash decisions often led to terrible consequences.

The potential for misery simply wasn't worth the risk.

* * * *

Ivy's stomach roiled and pitched as she weaved and shuffled ahead of Cole and Mya en route to the suite. *Not...going to...make it.* She belched and gagged, reaching for the nearest potted plant to puke in for the second time since achieving her narrow victory. The man sitting next to her with the bratwurst hat had won the competition with a truly revolting twenty-one brats in the ten minute time limit, but all she'd had to do was out-eat Cole. She'd choked down fourteen brats to Cole's thirteen.

Or so the contest judge had announced.

She'd lost count at seven, and honestly, from the look on Mya's face, she wouldn't be surprised if his sister had somehow thrown the count. Especially looking at Mya's decidedly disheveled hair and flushed cheeks after coming out of the backstage area with the contest judge.

You little devil.

Ivy shook her head at Mya, who gave her two thumbs up. *Too much motion.* Ivy groaned, cradling the defiled pot to her chest as Cole slipped the key card from his jean's pocket and opened the door to the suite. He hadn't said a word since they'd left the village and arrived back at Castle Alainn. He was probably ticked, especially if he could read the not-so-subtle cues to his sister's duplicity. But unlike Mya's open-book expressions, Cole was hard to read.

Ivy glanced at him from the corner of her eye before escaping to the privacy of her bedroom. No sooner had she shut the door and settled in front of the toilet when it reopened to admit Mya, speaking rapid-fire Spanish.

"Little privacy here?" Ivy choked out.

"Oh girl, it's way too late for that. I've already seen you hurl your guts out, so I hardly think it matters anymore."

Ivy's stomach danced unpleasantly. "Your brother must be a very patient man."

Mya opened the narrow window and turned on the bathroom fan. "Are you really getting all prissy and proper while your head's hanging over the shitter?"

What Ivy wanted to tell her and what manners dictated she say were two very different things. So she kept her mouth shut to please both her parents and herself.

"Mya, *out*."

Ivy shivered at Cole's stern directive, but didn't dare turn away from the toilet bowl. Mya's protest ended abruptly, leaving silence in the wake of her footsteps. The bathroom door closed, and Ivy rested her arm across the toilet seat as humiliation flared hot and sticky to the surface.

Epic fail, Ivy.

How pathetic was this? No guy alive would ever want to spend a week with a woman who'd challenged him to a freaking brat eating contest, not to mention one who became a retching hot mess in the aftermath. *Oh my God.*

A warm hand on her back made her yelp. She spun around, then moaned as a new wave of yuck twisted in her belly. Jesus, *Cole* was still here?

"You sh-should go. I feel really...g-gross," she managed.

Cole didn't technically smile, but the warmth in his hazel eyes made her prickly skin relax slightly. "Firefighters are first responders. I handle gross all day long."

He filled a glass at the sink, passed it to her, then sat on the floor, leaning against the wall. "There's an elderly woman with irritable bowel syndrome who calls dispatch once a month, vowing she's dying. Every month, we go to her house, give her water, a fiber supplement, and an antispasmodic. A half hour later, she sends us on our way with homemade cookies."

Ivy laughed in spite of her misery. "Why do you keep showing up? My economics professor father would say it's a blatant waste of taxpayer money."

Cole handed her a cool, damp washcloth to wipe her face. "And what would *you* say?"

She glanced at him in surprise. It looked like he really wanted to know. "I'd say she's lonely. And that your fire station values human dignity."

He nodded. "When there's a true emergency, we know our priorities. We go when she calls because there might come that one time when she's actually in trouble."

Ivy could only stare. She'd already deduced that he was more serious than most other guys she associated with, but he was obviously kind and introspective as well. "You plan to honor your bet and stay here with me even though you think I'm a disgusting flake, don't you?"

"No."

"No?" she parroted like a fool.

"You're not a flake, and you're definitely not disgusting. I think you're suffering the effects of a massive dose of saturated fat and fearless enterprise."

She smiled and groaned at the same time. "Please go easy on the word 'fat' right now."

His eyes crinkled in the most appealing way, and she sighed, regretting what she had to say. "I release you from the bet. I'm sorry I manipulated things. I don't blame you if you're mad."

He cocked his head, considering her. She pushed away from the toilet, careful not to brush against his long legs. She rinsed the washcloth under the tub faucet instead of the sink so she didn't have to face him because she looked like a train wreck.

He waited to speak until she turned off the

faucet. "I accepted the bet. You won, and I never break my word. You'll feel better tomorrow."

Well, that was awesome, but did she really want him to stay simply because he was a man of his word? He'd made it clear earlier that he didn't want to be here with her.

The bathroom door rattled on the hinges. "Let me in! I can hear you guys talking in there, so I know she's not dying."

Mya.

Cole rose to his feet. "I'll track down some antacids and a bucket for you. If you feel up to it, park yourself on the couch. The Broncos are playing tonight. You watch?"

She nodded. God's truth, though, she'd watch ant races if he was sitting on the sofa beside her. "Thank you for being cool about everything."

He winked and left the room, hooking his arm around his sister, pulling her with him as he closed the bathroom door. Ivy could hear them talking in low tones in the living room for a short while before the suite door closed and a cozy silence blanketed the space. Her stomach was still unsettled, but at least she didn't feel in imminent jeopardy of spewing again. She pushed up from the floor, turned on the shower, and undressed in slow movements.

The warm water felt amazing. It was crazy how rinsing yuck away could rejuvenate your attitude. Maybe this week would work after all. To start, she'd have to figure out how to frame the brat story so it was appropriate for her fourth graders. Of course, they'd ask her about the competition's stakes. Motive had been one of their vocabulary words, and oh how she'd hammered the meaning and examples into their spongy little minds. For the last two weeks, 'motive' had been a constant buzzword in their classroom.

Why did the chicken really *cross the road, Ms. Ivy?*

Why do people get so serious when they grow up, Ms. Ivy?

Why do you have such a big tattoo on your back, Ms. Ivy? That one had prompted a parent call to the principal, which had resulted in a district-wide, employee dress code revamp.

Oops.

Why, why, why, Ms. Ivy? She loved all the whys and hoped the children would never stop asking. Hoped they'd never meet someone who had the power to make them feel like the *whys* weren't important. Because of the kids, she would continue to try new things, to put herself out there and fail and embarrass herself—over and over—because they needed more grownups who weren't afraid to ask the *whys* and *why nots*.

Time for a big dose of the *why not* medicine. If Cole said he'd stay, why not enjoy it?

Enjoy *him*?

She was drying off when someone knocked on the outer suite door. She looked around her bedroom but she hadn't unpacked yet. *Whatever.* She wrapped the luxurious towel around her and emerged into the living room. More polite knocking, so it couldn't be Mya. Maybe Cole had forgotten his key card?

Ivy peeked through the peephole. A cheerleader-type blonde in skinny jeans and a leather jacket stood in front of the door in the hallway, chewing on her lip. Ivy opened the door slightly. "Hi. Did you get locked out of your room?"

The blonde's eyes widened as she took in Ivy's wet hair. "I'm sorry. I must have...the wrong room..."

The way she said it made Ivy's stomach burble unpleasantly. "No problem. Have a nice day." She leaned back to close the door, but an UGG-clad foot slid into the door jamb.

"Wait! That looks like Cole's bag."

Ivy glanced down at the beat up black luggage with an embroidered *Poudre Fire Authority* insignia. She opened the door wider, hyper aware of the woman's sudden eagerness as well as her own spiked heart rate. Not good for a brat-fatigued gut. "You're looking for Cole?"

The blonde tried to peer over Ivy's taller shoulders. "Cole! It's Shelly!"

Ivy nearly shut the door in her sweet, perky face. "He's not here at the moment. What business do you have with him?"

The blonde's white-toothed smile was as perfect as her trendy outfit. "Business? No business, I'm all pleasure. I'm his girlfriend."

Five

Cole entered the suite and froze. Mya rammed into his back, her mouth blissfully silenced on a grunt. Ivy's bedroom door stood slightly ajar. Enough to let him drink in the sight of her curves in gorgeous profile as she drew a scrap of fabric up the long, smooth length of her legs. The blue lace came to rest at the flare of her hips. His gaze roamed higher to the soft plumpness of her breasts with their pink peaks. The blood pulsed in his groin.

Ivy turned, caught him staring. *Joder!*

She covered her breasts with her arm and slammed the bedroom door as Mya poked him in the back.

"Been awhile *obviously*." If anyone could deliver a smirk in their voice it was Mya.

Cole took a deep breath, set the bucket he'd

found on the floor by Ivy's door, and took a seat on the sofa. He'd detected hurt in Ivy's expression for the brief moment they'd locked gazes. He sifted back through their earlier conversation in the bathroom to figure out what he'd said or—

The toilet flushed from *his* side of the suite.

He and Mya exchanged looks. He stood, and as he approached the door to his bedroom, it opened. His heart stopped.

"What in the *Sam HELL* are you doing here, you spoiled diva?" Mya yelled, adding a string of colorful Spanish curses.

Cole caught his sister in a chest hold before she could assault his ex, hardening his heart against the happy tears that formed in Shelly's eyes.

"Oh, *puh-lease*! You're not going to fool my thick-headed brother again with that fake-ass crying!" Mya squirmed in his arms, but he tightened his hold. "Let me go, *cabrón*."

Shelly reached her hands toward him beseechingly. "I'm sorry, Cole. I was so overwhelmed trying to help my brother when he came home. I shouldn't have pushed you away, I should have turned to you."

"Liar! You dumped his ass because after Stan died he was sad for a little too long!"

"That's not true!" Shelly cried.

Cole heard Ivy's bedroom door open. Mya wrenched out of his arms and went to stand belligerently next to Ivy, who now wore clothes and a carefully neutral expression.

Shelly bit her lip, narrowing her eyes at Ivy before moving her gaze back to him. "Can we go somewhere else to talk about this?"

It was on the tip of his tongue to say yes. He'd always tried to please her, and for a long time, she had done the same for him. Maybe he owed her that much.

"You don't deserve any of his time! A good woman stands by her man when he's down. You ran the other way, *puta*!"

"Mya, enough!" *Dios*. He looked at all three women in turn. When his gaze found Ivy's, he saw an openness that dialed down the tightness in his chest. "We're not together anymore."

Ivy nodded and smiled faintly. Her face had regained its honeyed pink tone. He didn't know why he felt the need to confirm what she'd obviously gathered watching this fiasco.

He should use this as an opportunity to get

45

out of this contest. But that would be weak and unfair and...

He didn't *want* to.

Don't think about why.

He turned back to his ex where she'd remained surprisingly silent. "You need to go."

Shelly approached him slowly. "I understand if you need time. I've booked a room here for the week, so I'll be around when you're ready to talk."

"Are you kidding me?" Mya bellowed.

Shelly put a hand on Cole's arm. "I don't hold any of *this*," she paused to glance at Ivy, "against you. I want us to start over with a clean slate."

"You left me, not the other way around." His heart pounded as he moved toward the doorway.

When she joined him there, she smiled. "We want the same things in life, Cole. Everyone gets lost sometimes. I won't ever make the mistake of letting you go again," she cooed quietly, then pulled the door shut softly behind her.

He leaned against the wall and ran his hands down his face.

Mya's frown could melt steel. "Don't tell

me you think she's sincere."

"I don't know what to think right now, Mya. But it's time for you to go, too. This doesn't concern you in any way."

Why hadn't Ivy said anything? She hadn't even moved. If the situation was reversed, he probably would have been out the door right after the ex had shown up.

"You think you're entitled to know every little detail about my life, but you can't give me the courtesy of knowing who might become part of our family?"

"I'm not discussing this with you."

Mya cursed another Spanish blue streak. "Fine. You know what?" She marched up to him and sputtered. "Just...*oooo*! You are a colossal pain in my ass."

"Calm down, I didn't bring my defibrillator, *hermanita*. Scoot on out of here and enjoy my truck this week. If you scratch the paint again, it's coming out of your pocket this time."

Mya scowled at him and opened her mouth, but at his raised eyebrow she marched to Ivy and gave her a big hug. "Keep pushing his boundaries. If you can get him into bed, you'll open his floodgates. He's very affectionate once you—"

"*Fuck, Mya!*"

"That's what I'm talkin' about. Have fun!" She winked at Ivy, then left before he clobbered her. His hand closed around the door handle, his eyes shut as he tried to figure out what the hell to say. Shelly's arrival had obviously prompted the hurt he'd seen in her eyes. Hurt that had morphed into a neutral curiosity. He'd detected no judgment. That and her zest for life were profoundly refreshing. But before he could let himself get pulled in, he had to deal with his past.

Could he go back to Shelly? Did he even want to?

He slid a hand down the heavy wood door and finally turned around, hoping to have his answer when he looked at Ivy.

But the room was empty.

Six

Well, this sucked. Ivy paced in her bedroom for a few moments, trying to wrap her brain around what had just happened. Cole had told Shelly to leave, but whatever was between them certainly wasn't a done deal.

Damn. She shouldn't really care. It wasn't like she'd ever see the sweet and sexy fireman again after this week.

It would have been nice to have a fun, frivolous vacation, though.

She stopped at her suitcase and pulled out a picture of her students. It had been taken after their 'nice' pose—the one where they were all making funny faces. She couldn't bail on her documentary or her plan to face her fear of heights.

Don't forget about letting go of the guilt.

That was the biggie, really. The thought of disappointing her parents weighed her down. She was sick of it. She was an adult, for crissakes. She shouldn't have to feel guilty about making self-affirming decisions like her choice of occupation.

If only they could be happy for me.

She set the picture down, slipped on her hiking boots, then grabbed her vest and video camera. When she opened the bedroom door, Cole's hand was raised to knock.

He frowned at her vest. "You're leaving?"

"Do you want me to?" *Ivy, Ivy, Ivy.* That sounded way too...*relationship-y.*

"I..."

"Sorry, I...I thought I'd get some fresh air while you—you know—rearrange your brain or whatever guys do when women pour themselves all over you." She slipped past him. Even without touching him she could feel his body heat.

"Conway said the view from Eagle Lookout is nice. I could take you..." When he trailed off, she glanced back, unable to erase the surprise that must surely be on her face. He appeared nearly as bemused. "It'll be dark in a couple hours, and I don't like the thought of you out there alone," he finished quietly.

Was this guy for real?

It was on the tip of her tongue to ask, 'what about Shelly,' but she didn't. *Not your business. You're here for your own reasons.*

Still though, what kind of fool was Shelly to cut this guy loose? Men like him didn't come around too often. *Enjoy the ride for however long it lasts.*

Maybe just an hour.

Monique would tell her she could do a lot of living in an hour. And an adventure to Eagle Lookout sounded like a good step toward conquering her acrophobia. Her pulse pounded in her neck when she pasted on a smile like she'd done a thousand times before. "I hope you can keep up."

* * * *

Cole had never been more aware of the way the setting sun cast gold-tinged shadows amid the yellow and orange canopy of the deciduous forest that he and Ivy wandered. Never more interested in the minutia of birch bark. Never more fascinated by the way a woman *moved* as

Ivy touched, smelled, and listened to her environment. She became part of her surroundings, losing herself in the wonder of nature's smallest details. The soft hoot of an owl, the quiver of a spider's web. It was all worth noting to her. All considered tiny treasures to celebrate and appreciate. She captured all of it on that little camera.

In the span of sixty minutes, Cole had learned a lot about Ivy. Perhaps most importantly, the high expectations imposed on her by her high-profile parents. She was an only child raised by high end nannies and Rhodes Scholar tutors. Her mother, a cardiothoracic surgeon at the University of Colorado's Denver hospital, while her father was an international consultant who taught economics at UC's Business School. It was easy to read between the lines that they'd had other plans for her besides teaching fourth graders in Grand Junction.

She used smiles and light sarcasm to disguise the hurt their lack of support caused her, but it was palpable in her body language. Her normally supple body tensed at his questions, her movements more rigid, her eyes full of shadows.

How differently they'd grown up.

Yeah, he'd learned a lot about Ivy Bradford.

And not nearly enough.

She still hadn't brought up his ex. He should be grateful. Instead, it left him at a loss.

He boosted her up to a foothold where she could climb the rest of the way up onto a boulder. He climbed up beside her, trying to stand close enough to block her from the wind without creeping her out. She seemed nervous, blowing out big breaths like she was winded and glancing at the trail below as though to reassure herself it was still there.

The air temperature had dropped significantly in the last fifteen minutes. So had the number of other hikers wandering the path. The view overlooking the resort and the village went on for miles, but the clouds had begun to roll in at dusk. "We should head back soon. Are you cold or hungry?" he asked.

She angled toward him, her gaze straying to his lips and then the trail once more. "My stomach's not ready for food yet, but you must be starving."

"I'm not overly hungry either." Though in his case it probably had more to do with his ex reappearing in his life than the thirteen brats he'd wolfed down a couple of hours ago. "Look, about Shelly—"

"You don't have to say anything, Cole. You're a do-the-right-thing kind of guy, but I don't want you to feel obligated to stay here because of me."

"Ivy."

"So I'm going to spare you the trouble and awkwardness and book my own room for the week. That way you can get your affairs figured—"

"*Ivy.*"

She blinked at him. "What?"

"Let's keep things as they are."

"Really?"

He nodded, trying not to dissect her preoccupied smile, because all of this was way out of his comfort zone. When he jumped down from their perch, she let out a little cry. He looked up as she squatted down to the boulder in exaggerated slow motion. From there, she eased onto her butt as far from the edge as possible, her fingers grasping at the tree roots sticking out from the rock.

Afraid of heights? He'd been so preoccupied about how to open the conversation about

Shelly, he'd missed all Ivy's cues. "You should have told me you don't like high places."

She wiped at a thin sheen of sweat above her lip. "I told my students I'd overcome my phobia. It's one of the reasons I'm here."

"That's admirable, but baby steps are usually better for this kind of thing." He held out his arms. "Come here. I won't let you fall."

"But I have to fall to land in your arms."

Her worried look made him want to chisel a staircase into the rock. "I promise I'll catch you."

With his encouragement, she scooted an inch at a time until her calves emerged over the edge. "I don't feel good," she murmured.

He reached up to run his finger along the canvas of her boot. "It's a short drop. I'll have your feet on the ground in no time."

She groaned, but scooted closer to the edge. "I have to close my eyes!"

"That's okay. I'll do all the work. Just let go."

"I'm too heavy!"

"You're perfect, *belleza*." He would know, he'd seen her nearly naked. He swallowed hard at the memory. "I know you can do it. Let go."

55

She did with a gasp. He caught her, holding her tighter than necessary. Her arms snaked around his neck, her face pale. "I bet women fall into your arms every chance they get."

He smiled. "My only reason for becoming a firefighter."

She exhaled slowly, the color returning to her cheeks. "Thought so. Put me down. I'm sure I'm a brick."

He didn't *want* to put her down. Not when her mouth was five enticing inches from his own. As he lowered her feet to the ground, however, her curves pressed into his body for several breathless moments before she moved away and started back to the resort.

"Why else are you here?" he asked after his pulse returned to normal.

"What do you mean?"

"You said overcoming your fear of heights was *one* of the reasons you're here."

One side of her lips lifted. "Let's just say I need a change."

Amen to that. Until he got here, he hadn't realized how badly he'd needed a life reset, too.

She used a mini flashlight from the camera bag at her waist to light the trail even though it wasn't fully dark yet. "Why did Mya enter you in the contest, why did you stay when you found out what it was all about...and why did Shelly walk away from you?"

There it is. The Shelly thing. "That's a lot of whys."

"It's a side effect of hanging around ten year olds all day long. You don't have to answer. It's none of my business anyway."

Her sincerity was like fresh rain after a drought. "Mya entered me because she wants me to be happy. I had no idea it involved sharing a suite with somebody, but it's hard to be angry with her when her motives are good. And when I won, I realized I needed to come here to just *be* for a while. I'm tired of over-thinking everything. I don't know what I feel for Shelly, but going back home with her isn't the place for me to figure it out." He ran a hand through his hair. "I realize how selfish that sounds. Sorry."

"It's fine. I didn't come here expecting a hookup, so why are we talking like this is a problem?"

Because it could be. She was intelligent, gorgeous, and fascinating. And they lived five hours apart. "Do you have someone in Grand Junction?"

He released his breath when she shook her head. "I've never really had a serious relationship. My parents always found something wrong with my dates."

That made him sad. "I'm sorry I...I couldn't take my eyes off you when I walked in and caught you...dressing..."

Her mouth opened without any sound. Christ, did he have to say it like that?

She waved a hand in the air, but her expression didn't look nearly as breezy. "Men and women can be platonic roommates, even when surprises like that happen." She nodded several times like she was trying to convince them both.

Well, good luck with that because hell would freeze over before any straight guy wouldn't think about sex with a roommate like her.

She put on another one of those it's-all-good smiles. "Tomorrow, I'm planning mountaintop yoga, fly fishing, then a wrap up at Oktoberfest where it's quite possible I'll enter the Stein Hoisting Competition. Wanna join me?" she asked. Her skin glowed by the string of trail lights as they approached the resort. She looked so hopeful, he couldn't ever remember wanting to kiss someone so badly.

He cleared his throat. "I'm no yogi master, but I'll try anything once."

Ivy stopped him, placed her hands on his shoulders, and leaned in for a quick peck on the cheek. "That's really sweet of you."

Sweet didn't come close to what he was feeling. Unsettled, restless, and as hard as these craggy cliffs was more like it. "Sweet? If my station heard you say that they'd tell you you don't know anything about me."

"That's okay. Deep's not my thing anyway. Besides, you don't need to know much about someone to have fun with them. Let's go, I'm suddenly starving." She started speed walking toward one of Castle Alainn's back entrances.

What had made her a *deep's not my thing* kind of person? He could see the deflective walls she put up to keep people from looking too closely at the emotions that hovered beneath the surface of her smiles, but she seemed dissatisfied with her facade. Like she wanted someone to authentically *see her*, but was afraid of it at the same time.

Ivy glanced back at him. "Get it out of granny gear, slacker! I thought firemen had to be in good shape to save the day."

A flame-engulfed room, the soot-covered girl unconscious in his arms as Stan's voice came through his helmet radio, 'I'm right behind you...'

A hand on his arm jerked him out of the past.

"Goodness, are you alright?" The concern in Ivy's eyes didn't bother him nearly as much as when he saw it in the gazes of his family and co-workers.

"Fine. I'm fine. Where do you want to eat?"

Ivy stared at him for a long moment. Her eyes held questions, but no pity. He let all the air out of his lungs and unclenched his fists.

Ivy's face relaxed in response. "I'm not usually a lettuce lover, but I think I'd better stick with something light tonight. So anywhere I can get a salad works for me."

Why hadn't she pressed him for answers? Everyone pressed. *Always.* "I think we can find something that'll work."

They had reached one of the resort's back doors. He started to open it when she stopped him with a hand on his arm. "I know your head's probably pulled in a dozen directions, but don't worry about meeting my expectations. Because I have none. Well, besides having fun. Think you can handle no strings with me?"

Hell no. He was a strings kind of guy. Strings were all he'd ever known. Heavy threads that bound him to his family, his career, his friends. Bindings that gave him roots and belonging.

And ulcers.

He stared at Ivy with her silky, untamed hair longer than he should, contemplating all kinds of carnal ideas. Then wondered if he still had that roll of antacids in his overnight bag. Were frivolity-induced ulcers as unpleasant as the obligation-spawned sort?

With Shelly and Ivy in the same place, he'd likely find out soon enough.

Seven

Cole steered Ivy through the boisterous, overcrowded pub. The absentminded little circles he made with his thumbs on the back of her hips revved up her already sparking nervous system. Was he thinking about Shelly? Why were his hands on her body when he'd probably spent the last couple of hours with his ex?

Goddang.

It had been an almost perfect day. Ivy had staggered from her room in search of coffee at eight-thirty this morning and discovered Cole on the sofa reading FLIRTING WITH DISASTER, the steamy, hilarious novella she'd finished in the wee hours of the night. The book had been in the gift basket the resort owners had arranged with chocolates and a bottle of wine. After she and Cole had retired to their separate rooms, she'd only planned to read for an hour, but between her overactive hormones and the story's *beauty and the beast* trope, the vicarious sex and romance were exactly what she'd needed.

Curiously, Cole hadn't seemed embarrassed to be caught reading a romance novel. Instead he appeared amused and interested, which was disconcerting for reasons she couldn't articulate.

He'd poured her coffee, and they spent all morning together. After lunch, her appreciation for fly fishing grew by leaps and bounds as he teased the fly across the river's surface, the warm autumn sun kissing his glorious forearms. Occasionally he glanced back over his shoulder, making sure she didn't venture too near the deeper waters where the current ran hard.

Memories she'd never forget.

After they'd returned to the lodge, they rented a Jeep at the concierge desk—*she should have* known *she needed wheels here*—and then...

Cole had politely excused himself.

He didn't say where he was going, and she hadn't seen him until twenty minutes ago when he'd returned to the room as she was leaving for the village.

The heat from the partygoers paled in comparison to the thermal energy radiating from his body along her backside as they pressed their way further into the pub.

"You're tense. Sure you want to do this?" His lips moved in the hair behind her ear as he leaned in. She closed her eyes to drink in the sensation. When she nodded, his hands tightened ever so slightly and pulled her closer. He guided her around various drunken obstacles toward the line at the stein hoisting registration table. It made her almost wish Shelly would walk in, see them together like this, and gracefully leave the state.

Maybe the country.

How selfish can you be, Ivy? That would be exploiting Cole's chivalrous nature. He was a protective sort of guy. He'd be attentive to *any* woman he accompanied in this type of rowdy environment.

But man, he made everything seem so sexy and gallant in that quiet alpha way of his.

When they got in line to sign up for the stein hoisting competition, she swiveled to look at him.

"This crowd make you nervous?" he asked.

No, I just have trouble breathing around you. "I cut my crowd-tolerance teeth on rave parties during college. Trust me, this venue is tame."

Cole smiled widely. She wanted to lick those lips to see if they tasted as yummy as they looked.

"Good to know. I didn't peg you as part of the electronic dance culture."

She laughed. "I'm not. It was a one month rebellion following high school graduation."

"Why only one month?"

"To prove to my parents that I would turn out okay if I made choices they never would. Or so I told myself. It was more to convince myself that I could actually do something without their approval. Alas, I'm Catholic, and the guilt got to me. My two best friends tell me I have people-please-itis. Anyway, the rave parties got old rather quickly. Not to mention the hangovers and my fear of being busted by the cops."

The green shades dominated when his hazel eyes twinkled. "No documentaries of that period of your life?"

"Dear God, no."

A wide, square woman took the tiny stage in the corner of the pub, stuck both pinkies in her mouth, and whistled. When the crowd quieted, she announced that the women's round would begin first. Cole followed Ivy to the bar where she collected a large plastic stein and took a place at an elevated table along with about a dozen other women.

"Forty ounces, huh?" She'd be lucky if she could hold this bad boy up for longer than it took to sing the ABCs. She glanced down at Cole where he'd muscled his way to the front of the cheering section. "Any tips for me?" she yelled.

He cupped his hands around his mouth to project his voice. "Arm straight, back straight, and don't spill any beer."

She snorted. "Gee, thanks for regurgitating the rules. That'll definitely get me through, wise ass."

Cole cocked his head. "You want better advice? How about, don't quit your day job." His smile was the most natural one Ivy had seen on him yet. Her pulse kicked up a dozen notches. He really was disarmingly attractive in a boy-next-door-trapped-in-a-warrior's-body way. She had never met a man as nice or respectful as Cole. *That says a lot about the company you've been keeping.* "Keep that up buddy, and I'll tell your sister about your debacle at yoga this morning."

His eyes widened briefly before he broke into hearty laughter. When the elastic on his jogging shorts had failed during a basic yoga pose, she and several other appreciative women had learned he preferred going commando.

Thank you, downward dog.

For such a seemingly conservative man, it was a deliciously sordid piece of information that had distracted her all damn day. What other delightful secrets and erotic proclivities did he hide under that gentlemanly exterior?

In the end, Cole saw her through her first stein hoisting competition. She'd won second place and fifty dollars for her two minutes and twenty-one seconds of arm torture. Every time she had wanted to set that stupid mug down, Cole would mouth '*you got this*.'

Again and again, he made her feel like the only woman in the room.

While the men lined up to receive their steins, Ivy hustled for one of the tables down in front where Cole had parked for her round.

Someone jostled her, spilling some of her beer. A bearded man with a ponytail mumbled his apologies before moving off. The air was thick with too many bodies, and smoke from the patio wafted inside because they'd propped the pub doors open to dispel some of the heat. Ivy blew the foam off her beer and took another drink, enjoying the gritty humanity all around.

"Ladies, wish your men good luck!" the announcer yelled into her mic. Ivy set her beer down, took out her camera, and looked up to find Cole's beautiful eyes on her. She blew him what she hoped was a friendly, not-the-sexy kind of kiss. He winked back and she felt it down to her boot-clad toes.

No strings, Ivy. Just more beer. She picked up her mug.

He was a puzzle she didn't need to figure out because he was only in her life for one week.

Less if Shelly had her way.

The men raised their steins. Her heart rate elevated as the cheers and shouts began. Two minutes into the contest, Cole was holding up fine, but something was wrong.

With *her*.

Her pulse galloped and sweat ran down the

center of her back. She set down her stein and gathered her hair into a haphazard bun to keep it off her neck.

When it was down to Cole and one other competitor, Ivy couldn't bear to sit still. Her stomach curdled on her beer. *Must be sick.* Yet she didn't want to lie down like yesterday when she'd had too many brats. Instead she felt amped up. Like she could bust through these red brick walls.

Three and a half minutes into the competition, she paced along the outer edges of the pub, ready to scream. Everyone was shouting and cheering, and *ohmygod*, they needed to shut up!

A woman stumbled into her sideways and Ivy's tenuous thread of control snapped. She shoved the woman back.

Hard.

Someone with a deep voice bellowed and grabbed one of the wooden chairs with murder in his eyes. Ivy ducked. The air above her head stirred right before the chair splintered against the old brick wall. The place erupted.

Ivy kicked and dodged the man's punches. Fists and plastic steins flew around her. Her

69

mind was terribly fuzzy, making her see double of her attacker. His arm came toward her in slow motion. *That big, meaty fist is going to hur—*

Someone yanked her backward into a warm, hard chest. *Such a nice chest.*

Cole shepherded her toward the center of the room. "Get behind the bar. Don't fucking move until I come for y—" A sideways jab to his jaw silenced him.

Ivy launched at the bad man, jumping on his back, her arm winching across his windpipe.

"*Madre de Dios*, Ivy, *down*! Do you want to spend the night in jail?" He peeled her off the man, and carried her over his shoulder to plant her behind the bar. "Now *stay*."

"You're bossy!"

"And you're drunk and vulnerable," he growled.

She wanted to deny it, but her tongue was so thick and her throat so dry she couldn't get any words out. Cole moved away to help the pub staff get the most aggressive combatants under control.

So hot. Need air.

She looked around and found another exit sign at the back of the pub. Though her legs

70

wobbled, she could definitely run a marathon right now. She exited the pub, breathing big gulps of air. Where had Cole parked the rental car?

She walked and talked, asking people on the sidewalks if they'd seen the boxy little SUV. She couldn't remember what it was called. The strangers looked at her funny. Some even asked if she was all right, but she didn't know.

She suddenly couldn't remember anything.

Where am I?

* * * *

Cole pushed through the pub doorway, wiping the blood off his mouth as he looked both directions down the crowded sidewalks. His pulse, already jacked from the physical altercation, was a living thing in his neck. Sweat rolled down his temple and that suffocating pressure in his chest had returned.

This isn't life or death. He would find Ivy, and she would be okay.

Why the hell had he left her, though? He should have let law enforcement handle the brawl while he escorted Ivy back to the resort.

Something was definitely off with her. Her actions mirrored drugged behaviors he'd cared for when responding to 911 calls from nightclubs.

He took off, weaving between the window shoppers, then crossed the street and ran half way down the next block. Glancing down a narrow alleyway, there she was, talking to a brick wall. He reached for her, pulling her into his arms to reassure himself she was in one piece. She was shivering and sweating at the same time. He leaned back to observe her, but the alley was too dim to see her eyes. He took her wrist, feeling her pulse throb far too quickly. "Ivy, look at me. Did you ever set your drink down?"

"Well, yeah. It was a million ounces remember?" She squinted at him, then reached up to touch his face. "You are so gorgeous and you just...you don't even know."

"Let's talk while we walk, okay? How do you feel?"

"Lonely. I love my students, did I tell you that? Sometimes I think they're the only reason I'm not a casket base...Uh, basket race. Bashet cake? You know what I mean."

Basket case. "I do. They're lucky to have you."

She started bouncing and scratching at her arms with scared noises. He scooped her up and hurried the rest of the way to the busy street and better lighting. Then he stopped, put her down, and grabbed her chin to look closer into her eyes. Her pupils were extremely dilated. His heart pounded. It was so different responding to an emergency when you knew the person. "Listen to me, Ivy. Someone must have drugged your beer. I need to get you to the clinic so they can check you out."

"I need to move. I want you to touch me, Cole." She pressed herself against him. "You smell so good."

People around them were starting to whisper and point. He slung an arm around her shoulder and steered her toward the Jeep. "Do you have your wallet and phone on you?"

"Yep. See?" She held them up millimeters from his eyes, then shoved them back in her inside vest pocket and shivered violently. "Sooo itchy!"

"I'll take care of you. Hang in there, okay?" The clinic was on the edge of the village. They needed to figure out what she'd been given.

"I want to go skiing. The black diamond runs. Let's go now!" She began running in the direction of the ski lifts. He caught up to her, but she swung and screamed at him like she was being mugged. He took a few hits before he leaned down and lifted her in a fireman's carry across both shoulders.

"I hope you're taking me home. I pick your bed. That would be *so* much better than skiing because there's no snow right now. Did you know Colorado gets the most snow in March? One of my students researched that. She's so sweet. I wish I could take her home with me. I'd love her better than her meth-head mother. The way her momma treats her makes me want to cry, but I never do because that's not appropriate. I love my students."

Her hands skimmed down his trunk to his button fly, and Cole decided he was going to Hell because he craved her touch even when she was so fucked up.

They were almost to the SUV when a cop approached from across the street. "Mind telling me what's going on here?"

Cole set Ivy on her unsteady feet, clamped an arm around her to hold her up, then put out a hand for the cop. "Good evening, officer. I'm Cole Castillo with the Poudre Fire Authority, Station Four in Fort Collins. This is Ivy

Bradford. I believe she was drugged at Chumps while I was in the stein hoisting competition. I need to get her to the clinic, sir."

The cop shone a light in her eyes. "You her boyfriend?"

Right. This was going to look bad. "Second date." Not technically, but sitting in a bathroom while someone retched kind of launched you past first date bullshit.

The officer gave him a hard look before he spoke into the radio at his shoulder. When he was done, he glanced at Ivy again before staring at Cole. "ID, please."

Cole reached into his back pocket for his wallet. "I'll give a report, but can we do it at the clinic? I don't know what they gave her—some kind of stimulant—but the sooner I get her there, the sooner I know she'll be okay."

The cop's chin rose as he processed the situation. "She's not the first victim. We've had four women drugged in the last three weeks."

So it was probably random. A predator fishing for someone whose date or friends didn't have her back. *Sick bastard.* "What were the others given?"

The cop frowned like he realized he

shouldn't have said anything about it in the first place. A second cruiser pulled up next to them. The officer opened the back door. "Get in. I'll take your statement at the clinic."

Two hours later, Cole ascended the staircase at Castle Alainn alone. The clinic decided to keep Ivy overnight. He'd wanted to stay, but she'd yelled at him to go. The nurses had advised him to leave so Ivy would settle down. She was in good hands, but...

This sucked.

When he turned down the hallway to his and Ivy's suite, Shelly was sitting by the door. His shoulders tensed immediately.

Shelly quickly rose to her feet. "Thank goodness! You haven't been returning my calls. I was worried. Where's the girl?"

The girl. She didn't even have the decency to say Ivy's name. He didn't look at Shelly as he unlocked the door. "I'm tired. I'll talk to you later."

She pushed her hand against the door before he could close it. "Something happened. I'm not leaving until you tell me what it is."

He believed her, and he felt too guilty about Ivy to let himself be rude to anyone else right now. "Someone drugged her drink at the pub. She'll be alright, but they're keeping her at the clinic overnight."

"I knew bar hopping was dangerous. Some women take unnecessary risks like that. Can I come in and make you some coffee?"

He blocked the door and looked at his ex. A future with her would be comfortable, safe, and predictable.

Life with someone with as much zest as Ivy would never be that.

He didn't know what he wanted right now except silence. "I'm going to turn in now."

Shelly's smile faltered. "Will you join me for breakfast? They probably won't discharge her until mid-morning or later if her tests take longer."

"Fine," he said because he just wanted her to go. Once upon a time, he'd thought he wanted a life with her. But when Stan had died, maybe his buddy had taken pieces of him to the grave. He had been emotionally lost for six months.

Maybe longer.

Maybe since Dad's murder.

In that time, he'd learned that Shelly had the 'in good times' promise down much better than the 'in bad times' one. Of course, she'd had a lot to cope with, too; especially her brother's PTSD after his third tour in Iraq. People's worlds became much smaller when tragedy struck. And everyone dealt with it differently.

Cole stepped back and closed the door without another word. He walked through the darkened room toward the window overlooking the mountains. Their timeless, rugged outline stood out against the milky September sky.

Man was so small compared to all that rock.

So small and self-absorbed. All the masks people wear to disguise how much they were floundering inside. All the facades to hide their rough edges when people should really be more like those mountains. Unapologetic in their stark, raw state. Life would certainly be less complicated that way.

Probably less lonely, too.

Cole turned from the window and looked toward the shadows in Ivy's room, recalling her unfiltered words about her own loneliness and her love and compassion for her students. For all her casual smiles and social engineering geared to keep people from seeing the true Ivy, there was something deep and honest about her that he connected with.

He walked to her doorway, her scent—something citrusy and bright—hitting his nose. The tension evaporated from his shoulders. He stood there a moment before walking back to the living room. He pulled his cell phone from his pocket, sank into the chair by the fireplace, and called the nurses' station.

He was tired, but he wouldn't sleep until he made sure Ivy had settled for the night.

Maybe not until he figured out what to do about the holes in his life that had been laid bare by a leggy school teacher who'd brought the sunshine back into his world.

Eight

Ivy shaded her eyes against the sunlight as the clinic's automatic door swished open. She took a deep breath, then winced as a sharp pain shot through her head. She had imagined this week would be memorable, but had never anticipated recovering from a massive caffeine overdose.

Someone had spiked her beer with something like four or five thousand milligrams of powdered caffeine. A potentially lethal dose in one small teaspoon, according to the Noble Pass Police.

Maybe the universe was telling her to go home.

Then Cole, in all his gorgeous seriousness pulled up to the curb in the Jeep, and she told the cosmos to piss off.

His eyes never left her as he exited the rental and ran to where she stood holding on to the back of a bench. "The nurse said you were being discharged at eleven."

She smiled at his frown even though it made her skull feel like slalom skiers were using it for ramp practice. "I decided ten thirty was better."

"How are you feeling? I checked on you last night..."

"I heard." The nurses had swooned like schoolgirls over him. "Thank you. I'm okay, but a little unnerved about some of the things I think I said."

It was his turn to smile. "Getting doped will put anyone into overdrive."

Oh, damn. That meant she'd been as horny as she'd thought. *Doesn't mean I didn't mean what I said.* Not that she'd ask him to go to bed with her. He wasn't the kind of guy you asked. If he wanted you, you'd know. Man, though, she was a raging hormone around him.

It had been too long.

Or maybe it was just Cole. "Thanks for preventing me from causing a full-scale riot last night."

He nodded. "Ready to go?"

She looked over at the Oktoberfest tents in the center square. "Mind if we come back after I shower? I need some fresh air, plus I want to purchase a few things to bring back to the classroom. Show and tell is a big deal, you know."

Forty minutes later when they approached a tent filled with traditional German attire, Shelly stepped out with one of her cheerleader smiles.

You've got to be kidding me. Maybe the universe had a sick sense of humor.

"Hi, Ivy, glad you're okay. I heard you were drugged. Good thing it wasn't Ecstasy."

Ivy's gaze cut to Cole before turning back to Shelly. "How do you know what happened?"

Shelly batted her eyes at Cole, then blinked at Ivy with challenge in her gaze. "Cole told me over breakfast. Did you know he hates orange juice and likes his omelets with ham and tomatoes? He enjoys jazz, Eric Clapton, and Bach."

"Shelly, stop," Cole warned.

She didn't even look at him. "He broke his arm getting my sister's cat out of a tree, and he was quarterback of the football team until he gave up all school extra-curriculars to get a job to support his family when his dad died."

"That's enough."

Ivy laid a hand on Cole's forearm, which felt like iron under her palm. "It's okay. I think anyone would be stupid not to fight for you."

Cole's gaze bored into hers. "She dumped me, not the other way around."

That's what scares me. Ivy looked at Shelly, and as much as she wished it wasn't there, she saw love on his ex's face. "We all make mistakes. But we have to live with the consequences when poor decisions are made."

Shelly slipped an arm around Cole's waist. "She doesn't know what she's saying, baby."

Cole's swarthy face had paled. *What did I miss?* "I was talking about *you*, not him," Ivy said.

"Of course you were, dear," Shelly patronized. Her other hand crept onto Cole's chest, but he pushed it off and turned away, running his hands through his dark hair.

Seriously, what had just happened? "Hey, I don't want to come between you two, so I'll do my own thing this week, alright? I'll get a cab back to the resort. You guys just..." she waggled her fingers at them, "do whatever it is couples

83

do to clear the air." Was it depressing that she didn't know what that was? She'd never been in that type of intimate relationship. Hers were either hookups or buddy dates because she needed a plus one.

She walked into the tent, holding her breath and praying she didn't look as pathetic as she felt. She picked up an overpriced pair of *lederhosen*, blinking fast and hard.

She was being emotional and completely unreasonable. She hadn't come here expecting to meet anyone. Yet she was acting like she had some kind of claim on Cole after a couple of days. *Dumb, dumb, dumb.*

He was just so...*different.* Different in all the ways that mattered. Yeah, she didn't know specifics about him like Shelly did, all his likes or dislikes, but she knew a lot of core things about him that made her care enough to *want* to learn the little things.

She added a cuckoo clock to her armload.

"I see we're going to have to make a trip back to the Jeep before we make fun of the polka dancers."

She turned to Cole slowly. Shelly was nowhere to be seen. Ivy exhaled deeply. "How do you know I love to polka?"

His eyes crinkled. "Do you talk in your sleep often?"

Oh, great. "No way. What else did I say? Or maybe I don't want to know?"

"I'm just kidding. You didn't talk in your sleep. Of course, you've only spent one night at the suite. You have five more to unload your darkest secrets."

He laughed when she jabbed him with her elbow. He took everything from her arms and followed her to the next table. "Do you snore, too?"

She tried not to smile. "That's a rude thing to ask a woman."

"So, you *do* then."

"I do not! You'll find out for yourself toni—" *Ack.* He'd probably be in Shelly's room tonight.

He set her things on a table and took her hand. "This is awkward for both of us. I'm sorry, Ivy. I'm in no hurry to jump into anything with anyone, but I feel lighter and happier than I have in a long time. It feels good."

"I'm glad." Ivy traced the veins in his hand, unable to resist even the slightest opportunity to have both hands on him. "Mya told me a little about your friend Stan. If you want to talk about it, I'm here." Seeing the discomfort on his face, she pulled her camera out of her purse to give them both some emotional space. "In the meantime, we've got work to do. Can you hold that alpine hat next to the suspenders?"

After narrating her items for her students, she interviewed an Oktoberfest employee. When they emerged from the tent, Cole put an arm around her shoulders, squeezed, and let go. Moments later, a shiver danced down her spine, an uncomfortable chaser to the warmth of Cole's touch. She glanced into a candy shop across the street, and the cold look on Shelly's face left no doubt in Ivy's mind that Cole's ex had taken note of his brief affection as well.

And she was furious.

* * * *

Cole held Ivy's video camera as she polka danced with a surprisingly spry elderly man. The sun reflecting off the golden streaks in her hair weren't nearly as bright as her smile. She waved him into the sea of colorfully-dressed, bouncing dancers. Cole moved toward her, unable and unwilling to do aught but be swept into her current. He zoomed in on her face, her cheeks flush with the physicality of the dance, and her eyes, laughing and more open than they'd been all morning since their excruciating encounter with Shelly.

He'd never realized how shallow or controlling Shelly could be. Maybe he'd just never reflected on their relationship. Thing was, once you noticed something, you couldn't un-notice it.

When the song ended, Ivy kissed her dance partner's cheek, then turned to bestow one on Cole as well. Cole stopped recording and lowered the camera, reaching for her before she found another partner for the next song. He snagged her wrist in one hand, putting the camera into the case at his waist with the other.

Ivy's eyes twinkled. "Change your mind and want to polka?"

"Nah. I'm more of a cha-cha or salsa guy."

"Is that so?"

He shrugged. "My mom's Cuban."

"Ooo, I'd love to cha-cha with you."

He'd love to cha-cha—*and more*—with her."Oktoberfest isn't exactly the right venue."

"Now there's an understatement!"

The way her eyes sparkled was so addicting. He took a deep breath. "I'm telling Shelly to go home."

She blinked. "Why would you do that?"

"I want to be here. With you. I'm tired of feeling guilty about it."

"You shouldn't feel guilty. It's okay to be with someone who doesn't need you, Cole."

It was his turn to blink. He replayed her words over and over until she snapped her fingers in his face.

"Hello? Your blood sugar low or something?"

"No," he murmured. Instead, her words had released a high in his blood. A new awareness. She was little more than a stranger, but somehow she'd nailed his whole dysfunction—something he hadn't been able to see in himself for the last ten years—in one sentence.

It's okay to be with someone who doesn't need you.

For a decade, he'd been the fixer. The protector. The provider. The one with all the answers, even when he had to fake it. It had been a role that sat easily on his shoulders because he was self-aware enough to recognize that was his basic personality. He derived a lot of his self-worth from how well he provided for others.

What he *hadn't* realized was how it influenced his choice of friends, his occupation, his girlfriends—people or situations that were broken, in danger, or in need of stability.

It doesn't have to be that way.

Amazing.

"Cole, you're starting to worry me. Are you okay?"

His fingers slid into the hair at the nape of her neck. When his lips touched hers, the music, the dancers, the smell of the fry bread and sauerkraut from the street vendors, faded away. All he could feel and smell and taste and hear was Ivy. Her breath, warm against his mouth, the silkiness of her hair, the tiny gasps she made as electricity arced between their skin.

Her fingers curled through his belt loops as she leaned in. His heart thundered when her palms slid up his hips, lifting the edges of his button-up shirt. The brush of cool air penetrated his fog of desire. He nipped at her lower lip one last time.

Someone was hollering.

He drew her to the shelter of his body, glancing up to see what was going on.

The music had stopped. The dancers surrounded them, cheering and clapping with smiles and sly winks. Cole's face heated. Ivy turned in his arms to face the crowd, giving two thumbs up. The dancers erupted in laughter and more cheers.

The music began again, and Ivy pulled him along for two complete circles of the street's dance arena before Cole steered her away from the throng. Together they ran laughing down the street, past the face painting, beyond the last of the street vendors, almost to the corrals where you could buy an afternoon on horseback to the top of the mountain.

Finally. A quiet copse of trees. He drew her close and kissed her before she could fully catch her breath. Before he could reason himself out of why this was a bad idea. Why it was foolish and risky and...

Heaven.

Her tongue met his without hesitation. His hands gripped her ass, then slid up underneath her sweater, his palms tracing the contrasting contours of her hips and waist. Higher. Her hand fisted in his hair, pulling him closer, her tight body flush with his. He reached down and grabbed underneath her thighs, wrapping her legs around his pelvis to grind against her. Her neck arched back, the sexiest sound he'd ever heard spilling from her lips.

And oh, how he wanted her. A rich, dark flood of lust heightened by the simple remembrance of what it felt like to live without the goddamn ever-present guilt.

With Ivy, he was free.

With her, risks felt worthwhile.

Ivy's breath shuddered next to his ear. "Let's go back to the suite. Or somewhere on the trail we found that first night."

His body screamed for release. He let go of her thighs, his fingers curling into her ass as she slid down his body to her feet. One more taste of her mouth before—

"Oh my God!"

Ivy pulled away, rearranging her sweater like she had all the time in the world and Shelly wasn't standing a few feet away, sputtering like a scorned lover.

And what the hell was Shelly's best friend Sabrina doing here?

"What's going on?" Sabrina shrieked.

"It's called heavy petting, or, for the more refined, *foreplay*," Ivy retorted.

Cole stepped forward to draw Shelly and Sabrina's angry attention away from Ivy. "Why did you follow us?"

Sabrina approached him. "Cole, you are the most loyal person I know. You don't do wild, irresponsible things like this."

"Sabrina's right. Come on, let's go."

He avoided Shelly's grasp. "It's sick if you brought Sabrina here to try to influence me. Pack up and go home, Shelly. I'm not interested in picking up the pieces of our broken relationship."

"You're letting hormones cloud your better judgment. You're smarter and more mature than this," Shelly argued.

Ivy stepped in front of him like she would protect *him*. "Would you give him a damn break with all the lectures? I don't know anyone else who has shouldered the responsibilities he has, much less become head of the household at sixteen years old. He sure as hell doesn't need a ball and chain like you to tell him what duty means."

Shelly's eyes practically bugged out of their sockets. "You bitch!"

"Callin' it like I see it, honey," Ivy said.

Cole put an arm around Ivy's shoulders. "Take Shelly back to Fort Collins, Sabrina. There's nothing between us anymore."

Sabrina shook her head. "She needs your support more than you know."

Shelly's eyes teared up. "We need to talk, Cole. *Privately.* I have something important to tell you. I wanted to wait until we'd cleared the air about some other things, but this can't wait any longer. What I have to tell you will change your life."

An unpleasant shiver skated down his spine. "There's nothing else I have to say to you." He took Ivy's hand, heading where he'd parked the Jeep in the village, feeling Shelly and Sabrina's stare like a target on his back the whole way.

"Some vacation, huh?" Ivy said quietly.

"It's not boring." He tried to shake off the clamminess caused by Shelly's parting words. Dread hung over him as he replayed them in his mind.

What I have to tell you will change your life.

Shelly seemed unstable. Over the last several days, her behavior bordered on stalking. Other things about her were off, too. But she was alone. Besides Sabrina, she couldn't depend

93

on anyone. Her mother suffered from debilitating mental illness, her brother wrestled with his own demons, and her self-absorbed father and younger sister were on the other side of the country. Who would help her?

He glanced at Ivy. Her expression and body language communicated calm. He wished he knew what to say to apologize for the drama he'd brought into her life. For a moment, he'd let himself be reckless. It was incredible. But every time he let instinct overrule his head, it ended badly.

Ivy's wide blue eyes fixed on him when he opened the passenger door for her, but he couldn't bear to let her see his confusion. Let her see that he didn't have the answers.

When they returned to their suite, he turned on the gas fireplace. Ivy removed her coat, her breasts pressing against the thin weave of her sweater. When his eyes finally tracked up to her face, she was smiling.

"How can you be happy right now?" he asked.

"I've never had someone choose me."

"More the fool they."

She walked toward him. His body tightened.

"You know how to make a girl feel special."

He stuck his hands in his pockets so he wouldn't reach out and grab her. *Now what?* "I'm sorry to drag you into this mess. Sorry I wasn't watching and you were drugged. *Mierda.*" *Don't come any closer.*

She smelled like ocean waves and skydiving and passion.

It made the reckless in him batter against the walls of his better judgment.

Ivy cocked her head like she was trying to see inside him. "I'm responsible for my own liquor, and it's not surprising that your ex wants you back. None of this is the end of the world."

He took two steps back to her step forward. "You make it sound so easy."

"Why can't it be?" she asked.

"Because...*you*. I *like* you." Memories of her would stay with him long after this week was over.

"I don't do strings, Cole. I've already told you that."

"I know." *Madre de Dios*, that should have been a green light to toss her on his bed like his dick was urging him to. Instead her 'no strings' proposition pissed him off.

"Then what's the problem?"

"Strings are all I know," he barked.

She smiled as her hands went to his button fly. "Then it's time you had a new teacher."

Nine

Warning bells rang concurrently with the surge of desire pulsing through Ivy, but there was no way she was passing up the chance to be with this man if he'd have her.

His hands engulfed hers on his button fly. The fly that constrained a very nice bulge beneath the denim. "I can't do this, Ivy," he said hoarsely.

"Sure you can." She skimmed his fingers under the edge of her sweater. His eyes darkened. Her heart throbbed against her ribcage. "You run into burning buildings for strangers. What can you possibly be afraid of?"

His fingers curled into her skin before he shifted them to her upper arms. His hands squeezed like his control hung by a thread. "You

97

make me feel things I shouldn't."

"I don't understand."

"You see beneath the surface, drawing me out into the deep end. Yet you try to keep everything so casual. You can't have it both ways, Ivy."

She backed out of his grasp. "This isn't about me."

"It sure as hell is. You see the wild and reckless inside me—the parts I try so hard to keep on a leash. But around you, I can't seem to find restraint." He sank onto the sofa.

"That's no way to live, Cole."

"It is when all I do is hurt people when I let it out."

Whoa. This was getting heavy. She barely knew Cole. Usually when guys got all confidential on her, she bailed. Or used more pleasurable ways to distract them. She forced a smile and sashayed to him. "I didn't know you could be so melodramatic."

He tunneled his hands through his hair and got up to walk to the window. "I refuse to argue with you. All this is crazy. I don't know what I'm doing here. I don't even *know* you."

But he did. In three days, he understood

things about her that most people never took the time to see. "Do you *want* to?"

He stopped pacing to pin her with a hot look that dried her throat. "Want to *what*?"

Oh, the possibilities in that question.

He made her utterly wanton.

She inhaled slowly, too terrified to actually explain what she'd been referring to. To ask if he wanted to see inside. *Why would you even do such a thing?* What would be the point? They'd part ways and never see each other again.

Then again, maybe that *was* the point.

Masks were ineffective once you let someone *in*.

Ivy Bradford on a 'B' day wasn't witty or charming. And no matter how many birthdays came and went, the one thing she could never quite outrun was the desire to not disappoint.

But she didn't live in the same zip code as Cole. She could come clean with him about her truths because there would be no long-term consequences. She could be open and vulnerable without worrying about him holding shit over her head or living with his disappointment because he'd be nothing but a memory in a few days.

This time, Cole approached *her*. Real slow, like he wasn't even breathing. Just watching her every move. "I said, *want to what*, Ivy?"

Get to know me. The real me. "Do you want to try being a different way? Not all adventurous choices have bad consequences."

He picked up her hand and placed it on his chest. "No, but in my experience, when they do, they're devastating. It's not worth the risk."

His chest rumbled under her palm. She loved the deep resonance of his voice. Could listen to it all night. She'd replayed it over and over these last few days until it followed her into her dreams.

She raised her gaze to his as his words finally penetrated. *Not worth the risk.* She backed away, trying not the let the hurt show. He followed as though pulled by invisible threads. She couldn't let any of her relationships progress to the point that real feelings were involved.

And he didn't trust the consequences that might result if they dropped their masks.

Not worth the risk.

Her toe in the pond of vulnerability...
...rejected.

Hide. Before the glitter rubbed all the way off. "I totally get it." *You don't want me.* "I'll freshen up and grab supper at the buffet downstairs. Then it's on to keg bowling. The kids will think it's a hoot. Of course that might get me in trouble with the district again so I may end up editing—"

"Ivy."

He closed in again, making her heart pang and her hands rise defensively. "Sorry, rambling again, right? I'll just, I'll..." she pointed to the door, "go now."

God.

She turned away and heard him swear under his breath. His hand grabbed her belt loop, stopping her in her tracks. She swiveled back and found herself exactly where she'd wanted to be since he'd walked into her bedroom with his sister that first day.

In his embrace.

"What is it about you that makes me defy all good intentions?"

His mouth covered hers before she could wind up for a cheeky comeback. Everything lush and stormy inside her unfurled. She jumped up to wrap her arms and legs around him. The

101

inertia barreled him back into the sofa arm. They tumbled down onto the cushions, a delicious tangle of limbs, Cole's arms tightening around her as they fell. She bounced once against his chest as they came to rest. He laughed against her mouth, a vivid, beautiful sound. "You okay?"

She nuzzled his neck where his pulse beat strong and warm. "Not quite. You see, I have this terrible ache." She rolled her hips against the glorious ridge in his jeans, eliciting a groan from them both. "I can't seem to fix it by myself."

He found her hands to entwine their fingers. "Look at me."

Don't do it.

But dammit, of course she did. Her galloping heart revved higher. "Don't think so much. Jesus, most guys lose their ability to compose sentences by now."

"I don't know if I can make love without strings, Ivy."

Oh my God. Why did he have to go and say things like that? She looked at the swarthy hollow at the base of his neck and almost lost her nerve. "Then don't. Let's have sex instead."

His whole body stilled. He was gonna refuse. She held her breath. And then he sat up, bringing her with him in his lap. He stripped off her sweater, then shoved a hand in her hair to bring her mouth to his.

He kissed like he did everything else.

With earnest intensity.

Intoxicating.

She had to feel his skin. She leaned back to unbutton his shirt, marveling at his bronzed chest, the dynamic contrast between her softness and his strength. She ran a finger from his neck to the thin trail of hair that disappeared into the waistband of his jeans. "You should be painted," she whispered.

He stood with her in his arms and walked into his bedroom. She swallowed back a surge of unease. Going into his room felt too personal. But she pushed her nerves aside when he drew back the covers and laid her on the bed. "And you, *cariño*, shall be worshiped."

He wasted no time stripping off her jeans, kissing his way up her body until he lay flush against her in the most thrilling way. Her hands explored the warm texture and planes of his torso. Flames from the double-sided fireplace cast moving shadows on the walls as he slid halfway off her body, using his hand to stoke her fire higher. His fingertips glided across the tops of her breasts leaving goose bumps in their wake. His lips—my God, those sculptural lips— hovered above the lace of her bra, blowing softly across her sensitive skin until she couldn't hold still, craving more contact.

Open-mouthed kisses pulled a deep cord of longing through her pelvis. His hand splayed over her belly, one leg pinning her lower body to the bed. She explored the front of his chest, then unzipped his jeans and she found what she was looking for.

A guttural sound arose from his throat.

When he pulled back, she nearly clapped her hands in anticipation of no barriers between them. But he grabbed her arm and a leg and flipped her onto her belly, once again covering each part of her body with his corresponding flesh, the weight of him pressing her into the mattress. His denim-sheathed erection rocked into her thong-clad ass as he entwined their fingers on either side of her head. Her breath sawed in and out. His stubble pushed away her hair so his lips could find her ear. "Sure you want this?" His gravelly voice ricocheted through her.

"Y-yes. *Yes.*" She wouldn't beg.

Yet.

He inhaled deeply. A pause. Then, her bra was off, he was on his back, and she was straddling his neck, her sex one excruciating inch from his lips.

The intensity in his eyes shot adrenaline up her spine.

"Grab the headboard."

At his command, something dark and unfamiliar moved inside her. Her fingers curled around the cool metal of the headboard. Her blood pulsed hot and thick in her veins. His hands on her skin...dangerous...and safe...and perfect.

He cupped her breasts again before lowering his palms to her hips to slide her forward so he could kiss and nip the lace of her thong. Long, aching moments that were simultaneously satisfying and not nearly enough.

She looked down at his beautiful face pressed against her, her thong now a much damper shade of blue. "*Cole.*"

His arms came from behind her, ripping the flimsy thong in two so she was laid bare to him.

Her neck arched. So much to *feel*...The edges of her hair teasing her lower back. The carotid artery in his neck pulsing against her groin. The liquid strength of his tongue. Her legs spread wide, her knees pressed into the mattress, her hips rolling tight little circles against his mouth. His fingernails scoring the fleshy part of her ass as he intensified her movements.

He pulled back for moment. "Touch your breasts."

She did.

Felt. So. *Good.*

She moaned.

"*Ride it.*" The demand growled deep in his throat, vibrating against her skin.

A murky, back-room kind of joy built and expanded. Layers of sensitivity that left her breathless. Sparks behind her eyelids. Hands and mouth. *His.* Lips and tongue. All of it...

Hers

Exquisite.

Her mouth opened, unable to contain the fervor. Jolts of pleasure curled the edges of her consciousness outward to multiply the sensation. It went on and on until, breathless, her head rested against her arm propped against the headboard.

Oh. My. God.

She'd never...just...never...

Wow.

She shivered and shimmied down his torso until they were eye level. She'd meant to slide all the way down his body to dispense with his infernal jeans, but his gaze arrested her. She couldn't speak for the smolder in those hazel depths. She pressed her thumb against the wrinkle in the center of his lower lip, and he opened to her, lifting his head to meet her kiss. She kept her thumb on the edge of his lips, the sensation of his mouth moving, her taste on his tongue rekindling the ache between her thighs. He rolled her over slowly, then backed away, standing to dispense with the rest of his clothes.

"Finally," she said, her voice barely audible.

He smiled that smile that was somehow unbearably sweet, yet so wicked all at once. A part of her panicked at the thought of letting him inside her body. She'd told him no strings, so he knew the deal, but down deep, did she? *Of course, stop acting like a damn virgin.*

He had the most amazing shoulders and abs. They contracted and rippled like they had a life of their own as he stepped out of his jeans. She could watch him all day. She settled more comfortably against the pillows that smelled like him. A smell that made her go soft all over.

Soft and vulnerable.

No strings!

Adrenaline shot fire through her spine. She sat up abruptly, wrapping her arms around her legs. "This is just sex," she blurted.

He paused, regarding her carefully. "Okay," he finally said.

But she had a feeling he didn't believe it either.

* * * *

She was more skittish than any of the terrified animals he'd rescued in all his years of service. She wanted this, he was certain of it. But sometime between when they'd torn down the wall of their restraint and his artless strip job, her brazenness had faltered. Why?

He sat on the end of the bed and took her feet in his lap, massaging them until the tension melted from her legs. Gorgeous, smooth legs that nearly made him babble like a fool. How many months would he remember the feel of her thighs against his cheeks? The sounds she made as she came? "I don't want to do anything you don't want to do." *But I may have to take a very long, very cold shower.*

She blew out a breath and tucked her legs under her as she rushed to put her hands on his cheeks. Her ardent blue eyes unnerved him.

"You can't imagine how much I want you."

"I think I can," he whispered back.

She smiled. *Holy hell. So sexy.*

Something large and possessive and beyond words rose up in him. He pushed her back against the pillows and followed her body down, touching and tasting with his lips, skin, fingernails—soft, then hard, then soft again— until her lips parted with those sounds he could never tire of hearing. She gasped when his tongue dipped in her bellybutton. Then again when he nuzzled the underside of a breast. "I think we should have another rock climbing test tomorrow." He laved first one, then the other nipple. Her skin pebbled with goose bumps.

"Are you serious? How can you do, *ahhh*, *that* and still be coherent?"

Her rapid breathing, flushed cheeks, and grasping hands tested the limits of his control. He inhaled slowly. "Firefighters are good multitaskers."

But it was only true until she shifted her legs under him. He dropped between her thighs and suddenly her wetness cushioned his erection. They both moaned. He gritted his teeth, rolled away to suit up, and was back on top of her in a flash.

This time in her arms, there was no more talking.

His mouth fused to hers as her hips opened, her heels against his ass, urging him on. He pressed into her slowly as sweat gathered between his pecs, down the center line of his spine, fighting the pull of biology to drive home hard. *Please her.*

When he'd seated himself fully, he leaned up on his elbows to look at her.

With her, he had to *see*.

It had never been that way.

But Ivy was so expressive, it was another layer to enjoy. Another reward. Her mouth was open, but she was holding her breath, her brow troubled until he began to move. Her neck arched, and he couldn't help but brush the lock of hair from her mouth. He moved above her, sliding in and out, watching the thrilling nuances chase across her features. When her eyes fluttered shut, he kissed her soft lids.

Her arms wound around him like she wouldn't let go. Her breath ragged with primitive sounds against his neck. Her body tightened exquisitely, her fingernails driving into his back as the orgasm lanced through her. "Fly with me," she rasped.

He did. Explosively.

And when they both came down, he knew it would happen again, regardless of Shelly's forthcoming revelation. He couldn't hide from his ex's announcement forever, but it damn well wasn't going to be tonight.

Ten

Ivy shifted for a better camera angle at the wiener dog derby, grateful for Cole at her back, keeping the other spectators from jostling her. He had no clue how distracting his body heat was, and she had no plans to tell him, otherwise they'd end up back in their suite.

In bed. Or in the shower.

Or on the floor.

Oh hell, maybe they'd christen the trail on the way back to the resort.

A flush spread from Ivy's cheeks down her neck where she felt its warmth pour across her chest.

Wow. Focus, Ivy.

The dachshunds' long, pink tongues flapped and their smooth brown ears streamed all the way to the finish line. When Cole's heat vanished, she turned around to see him pick up and return a child's ragged, stuffed giraffe. Her heart squeezed. He turned and caught her watching. His eyes darkened like they did when he kissed her. Last night they hadn't made it to keg bowling. They'd ordered room service and spent their hours talking, laughing. *Touching.*

There was so much more to touch than the physical aspect. How had she never known that?

Finally, they'd pulled both of the comforters from their beds and slept on the floor on the living room-side of the fireplace. Ivy had woken an hour before dawn to see Cole, naked, spread-eagled, the hard lines of this face softened in sleep. She'd watched the fire light play over his features, trying not to think about all of this too much.

She'd learned so much about him. Yet he'd not spoken of Shelly.

He'd awoken then, and the look on her face must have been too raw because he didn't say a word as he covered her body again.

They'd made love once more before the first fingers of orange and pink filtered from behind the mountains.

When the last of the dogs crossed the finish line, Cole pulled her to his chest, wrapping his arms around her. "Are you cold?"

"Not anymore."

He kissed her neck below her ear. "Good. You want me to film the next heat so you can be in front of the camera?"

"No, I think I'll keep all the focus on the dogs. The kids will talk about this for weeks."

He moved to stand beside her, tucking her under his arm. "I'm sure they will. Apart from the fact that you were born for it, why did you choose teaching?"

She opened her mouth, ready with her stock answer—that she was an overgrown kid herself—but he deserved more than a superficial response. "You know how I told you about my career-obsessed parents?"

"I'm sure being an only child made their scrutiny intense. Mya has said more than once she wishes mom and dad would have had ten more kids so they wouldn't have been so up in her business. Now she directs those comments to me."

"Your adolescence ended abruptly with your father's death. What you did was remarkable."

He tweaked her nose. "You were saying about your parents..."

"They wanted me to follow in one of their doctoral footsteps. Either an M.D., like mom, or a Ph.D., like my father. They have awards and wealth and charities named after them. I'm proud of them. But even though they showed up at my activities when they were able to, they weren't really there for me when I needed them. Does that make sense?"

He nodded. "So busy making a career legacy they didn't have time for family."

She looked down at her feet when an uncharacteristic prickling rose in her eyes. He folded her into a tight hug and kissed her hair. "That must have been terribly lonely. Especially since you had no siblings."

She couldn't believe they were talking about this. Monique and Kay knew her parents, but she'd never opened up about the isolation and deficiencies she felt as a kid. She'd told herself she was over it now, that she had a career she loved and that was enough to compensate for the loneliness, but here with Cole, she was discovering that old scars still had the power to hurt.

When he didn't let go, she felt unfamiliar

words rise to her tongue. "They barely noticed my attempts to get their attention with good grades. After all, that was expected. The first time I acted out, they were shattered. My mother had a migraine for a week, and my father shut himself in his study with a fifty-year-old bottle of cognac. I was so appalled I begged their forgiveness. Since then, it's been easier for all of us if I simply meet their expectations."

He frowned. "That takes a toll."

"We came to an understanding four months into my first student teaching placement. I had originally pursued elementary ed because I was going to be a child psychologist. But the first time I walked into that bright, chaotic classroom filled with those unfiltered and untarnished little people, I was hooked. I wanted to be the one who filled their minds with wonder and learning and an unquenchable thirst for the whys of life. But the truth is, they've given me so much more than I've ever given them."

"If I'd had a teacher like you, I wouldn't have looked forward to summer break so much. How did that fly with your parents?"

"I didn't tell them I was sending teaching curriculum vitae out with my applications to grad schools. When I landed my first teaching job, my mother told me I should cultivate more suitable friends, as my oldest ones were holding me back. Can you imagine the arrogance?"

Cole squeezed her in response. "What was the understanding you came to?"

Ivy looked at the smiling children around them. "All my life I tried to please them. It sounds worse than it was. But teaching was something that was just for me. It made me feel so alive. For the first time ever, I felt like I was right where I belonged. I told my parents they could either accept that I was happy being a garden-variety elementary school teacher, or they could no longer expect me to be their token child in the audience when receiving their next accolade."

"Just so you know, you're well above average." He slipped his hand under her vest to ride his fingers across her hips. "I'm glad they accepted your ultimatum."

Accepted wasn't quite the right word, but the next heat in the wiener dog derby was suddenly underway. After the top dog was crowned, they drove the Jeep back to the resort and walked two blocks to a tiny, exclusive restaurant nestled on the edge of Lake Noble. Over bourbon-marinated elk steaks, Cole tried to get her talking again, but without the crowds, she felt too exposed.

He seemed to understand why she kept turning the conversation to lighter topics. And amazingly, he didn't seem irritated or bored or disappointed. Instead, he opened up about the night he and his best friend Stan had responded to a fire.

"The call had come in from a thirteen year old girl who was home babysitting her two younger siblings. The flames had started eating through part of the second story flooring by the time we got the younger children out. The chief ordered all of us out, saying we'd try to reach the older girl with the ladder. But I could see her through the smoke. She'd collapsed from inhalation. She couldn't stay in that house for another minute." Cole's eyes were haunted, faraway. Ivy reached for his hand. He squeezed her fingers. "I told Stan to go, that I could take care of it, but he stayed because that's who he was. I scooped up the girl—she weighed nothing in my arms—and as I ran to the stairway, I yelled for him. I couldn't see him through the smoke, but his voice came through my helmet radio, *I'm right behind you, buddy*. Then I heard a loud crack..." His throat convulsed.

Ivy blinked back tears, wishing they were anywhere but here so she could hold him. "I'm so sorry, Cole."

"My reckless sense of invincibility is why Stan left a widow and three kids behind."

"Oh God, Cole. You can't blame yourself for his death. Stan had to know the risks of the job just as well as you. That girl lived because you didn't waste time getting the ladder in place. You wouldn't have left Stan's side if the situation would have been reversed, would you?"

"Of course not."

"Bad things happen. Stan or another fireman could have had a freak accident and fallen off the ladder, who knows? We can't control when it's our time to go. You'll always miss Stan, but you can't keep blaming yourself when you were only doing the right thing for that girl. You saved a life, Cole. That's beautiful. Use that beauty to help you heal."

They stared at one another over the candlelight. Something profound moved across his features and her breath caught. Then Cole cleared his throat, rubbed his thumbs over the backs of her hands, and finally released her fingers. They didn't say anything more until

119

their waitress brought their check.

Heavy. Stuff.

Part of her wanted to keep talking about it, and part of her wanted to run for the hills. Her heart felt soft and possessive, and mighty vulnerable.

After leaving the restaurant, Cole suggested they make a fire in the pit overlooking the lake. "Last one there has to light the fire," she yelled, anxious to put these scary new feelings in a box until she could dissect them later, alone. She dashed down the dim path that led to a more private area along the water's edge.

Like children, they raced to their destination. He let her win, but insisted she sit in the two-person Adirondack chair while he gathered blankets, wood, kindling, and buckets of water from the Castle Alainn attendant at the discreet shed tucked in a stand of Douglas fir trees.

Cole built a nice, steady blaze, looking serious and masculine in the most primal way.

"You're quite a boy scout," she murmured.

"Just because I get paid to put out flames, doesn't mean I don't know how to start a fire."

Oh God, so true. He'd started one in her, and she was pretty sure she'd be a pile of ashes by the end of the week. Her heart had started that distracting thrum while her breasts ached for his mouth.

She opened the blanket on his approach, but instead of settling next to her on the chair, he picked her up and sat down with her on his lap. Before she could speak, his hands disappeared under the blanket to unzip her jeans. One large, warm hand found her. His rough sigh next to her ear melded with her moan. "Fuck, Ivy. So wet. I've been dying to do this for hours."

"We can't—"

"No one can see with the blanket. It's up to you how noisy you want to be. I won't tell if you don't."

How could she refuse? After all, it was dark and cool and there was no one else around besides the bored attendant who couldn't see them unless he came out of his shack.

Staying quiet wasn't easy with Cole's clever fingers, though. He stroked and delved, always bringing her right to the edge before pulling back, building her desire to a painful threshold. "Cole, please."

"Open up and take more," he whispered.

She shifted, letting her legs drape wider over

his, feeling the firm ridge of his erection against the seam of her behind. She ached. He groaned softly as his fingers played her like a finely strung Stradivari viola until the stars in the dark sky seemed to burst and shower into a thousand fiery streams of light. Her hips rolled against his hand, her chin caught in his other palm as he canted a soft string of Spanish against her neck.

As her body quieted, he held her, stroking her belly. How was she going to pay him back for that? There was always the jet tub in her bathroom. Or sex on the mountain top. Maybe if they got up there before yoga class—

His chest rumbled on a low chuckle. "Your mind never stops, does it?"

She leaned up to swivel around. The light of the flames shone in his eyes. "How did you get so good at reading people? It's unnerving."

"My mother said I was her intuitive one. Most people can be if they quiet themselves and listen to what's *not* being said. The problem is, we often don't like what we hear. Or what happens when we follow our gut. You're different. With the exception of your parents' influence, you try to follow your inner voice and chase your dreams. So much passion, yet so much vulnerability behind your catch-me-if-you-can smiles."

God, he was sweet. But she didn't know if she *did* sweet. That might be kind of hard to forget.

Oh, who the hell was she kidding? *He* would be hard to forget.

She re-zipped her jeans and reluctantly rose from his lap. "You think I'm vulnerable? Clearly, you're trying to assuage your pride after I beat you here. It's okay if you're not as fit as you should be."

They both laughed at her bald-faced lie. "I'd challenge you to a *real* re-match, but I don't want to humiliate you," he said. When he stood up, she remembered how much she loved their height difference.

"Now the cocky firefighter comes out."

"You ain't seen nothing yet, *mamacita*." He used not one, but two buckets of water to douse their campfire. "I'll give you a ten second head start back to our room." He smacked her ass, and she took off, heart thundering from far more than the physical exertion.

Here was the real Cole. The one down beneath the heavy weight of responsibility and self-sacrifice he bore for the love and welfare of his family. Here he was—still protective, still controlled and sexy—yet...

Ooo. A little dangerous and a lot bold.

This time, he easily overtook her, grabbing her hand and pulling her along. She was laughing too hard to run anymore so he bent down and piggy-backed her the rest of the way to Castle Alainn.

People in the lobby stared, but he didn't give her time to do more than smile at anyone. She laughed as he dashed up the stairs and down the hallway, until finally, they reached their suite. In the room, he set her down, pushed her against the wall, and wedged a thigh between her legs.

"What's the rush?" she gasped.

His lips came down in answer. Tongues, teeth, palms. Tasting, nipping, sliding. Forceful movements, his control balancing on a thin wire. She loved that. She shoved him back, his dark eyes confused, cloudy with desire. She unzipped her vest and dropped it to the floor, then loosened her boot laces and toed them off. He shucked his coat and boots and took a step toward her.

She held a hand up, unable to suppress a smile. "Wait."

"Don't want to."

Her laughter bubbled up. "You sound like one of my fourth graders."

"Trust me, *cariño*, I don't feel like one."

They stared at each other for an endless moment. *I'm in over my head.* She shivered suddenly. Cole pivoted and turned up the fireplace, then dimmed the lights as she quietly freaked out, trying to talk herself down from full-blown panic. She was letting this guy assume superhero status because she'd had a ridiculous number of orgasms in the last forty-eight hours.

Jesus.

She turned some slow music on her phone and set it on the table. Cole leaned against the door jamb to his room and pinned her with his hawk-like gaze.

Why had she told him to wait? Waiting meant thinking, and she knew the man was deliciously deliberate.

Her distress must've shown on her face because he pushed away from the door, his dark eyebrows pulled down in concentration. Her heart jumped in her chest. Here he was, always ready to fix things. Always ready to bear the

125

load on his broad shoulders. Such beautiful traits. He'd be an incredibly attentive husband. A devoted father.

Her belly fluttered alarmingly.

Stop. Freaking. Thinking.

Before he reached her, she shimmied out of her jeans. He paused to watch, his face in shadows with the fire behind him, but she felt the intensity of his gaze.

She closed her eyes and let the music become part of her flesh, swaying and rolling to the beat until her insecurities took a back seat to the music, and she once again felt in control. She opened her eyes and smiled to see Cole on the sofa, his feet up on the cocktail table, hands locked behind his head. She wriggled her behind as she sank down in time with the music, then pulled her sweater overhead as she stood up once more. The sweater became her prop, sliding across her shoulders and between her legs as she flowed across the floor. When she tossed the sweater at Cole, he caught it with one hand, then brought it to his nose.

"I smell your desire, Ivy."

She couldn't have responded to his husky timbre if she'd wanted to.

126

No thinking.

She turned the music louder. Keeping her back to him, she bent from the waist, running her hands up her shins as she stood, slow, *slooow,* imagining they were his hands.

And then his palms really were gripping her hips, his groin hot and flush with her ass. She hadn't even heard him get up from the sofa.

"Me encanta tu culo."

She had only a vague idea of what he'd said—something about her ass—but in any case, it was dead righteous sexy. She felt loose and humid and entirely drunk, though she'd only had one glass of wine at supper.

He swayed with her to the music, sliding his hands up her sides, all the way to her shoulders where he pushed her bra straps down. She'd never felt a man's touch as feather-soft as when he ran his fingertips across the swell of her breasts. She shivered, feeling hot and cold at the same time.

He pressed a large hand into her midriff, holding her back against him as he took over the dance of seduction. She was helpless against his warmth, his strength, his brand as he pressed himself into the very heart of her. She lifted her hand, sliding her fingers up his neck, into his hair as their bodies moved to the provocative music. His palm crept south, teasing the satin edge of her thong down. Her breath came harder, her breasts rising on every inhale. His nails bit into the delicate skin of her pelvis. "You like my touch."

Too much. He felt her nod, goddammit, but he moved away, a rush of cool air where his body had warmed hers.

He removed her bra. She turned to face him, bare but for her black thong.

There was a rough-hewn hunger on his face as he clutched her bra in one strong fist.

Time for that unflinching control to snap.

The next song was perfect. She feathered her hands all over her body, as slow as she could manage with her heart a'gallop, ultimately tracing an agonizing path to her thong. She watched every restless shift of his body as she delved her hand beneath the satin.

He gasped louder than her when her fingers found her heat.

He grasped her hand, bringing her fingers to his mouth. Her core spasmed as he sucked.

"I don't know what you're doing to me, Ivy,

but by God, I like it."

"Good. I have a four-alarm fire, and I'm in need of relief."

He swept her into his arms, the room filled with flickering shadows, blurring as his long legs ate up the space. She landed with a bounce on his rumpled bed—the bed they'd disheveled only hours before.

She slid her hands between her legs as she watched him strip with a raw grace. Piece by piece his clothes came off, inch by inch his hard body was revealed. *"Hurry."* The single syllable abraded her throat.

More demands made their way to her lips as he finished sheathing his gorgeous length, but they were silenced as his body roughly pinned her down, his voice husky, his accent heavier. *"Tu me vuelves loca."*

Her heart pounded so hard she opened her mouth to try to breathe. His knee came between her thighs, pressing them apart. He leaned up, fingers trailing down her belly, and pulled her thong to the side to slide home.

* * * *

Cole ground his teeth as they merged.

Home.

The more times his body met hers, the more insistent the word grew in his mind. He and Ivy curled together as though of one flesh, aching to peel apart, but needing the movement to feed the desire pulsing, straining, desperate.

More.

His body drove her relentlessly. Up on his elbows, he watched her expressive face, the play of shadows intensifying the grip of her teeth on her lower lip. Now her mouth open on the sexiest sounds he'd ever heard. Made his heart drum, his chest expand, his muscles warm and tense.

Give her more.

"Cole..." Her nails scored his back, his ass. "Cole..."

"You're beautiful," he whispered, the faintest of sounds. Their bodies rocked together, faster, the pressure in his groin intensifying with his pleasure. He pressed his lips against hers and in that moment, she let go. Her body clenched, and he drove onward, pushing her harder until he wasn't able to hold on any longer.

His body seized, his vision blacking out the instant his orgasm burst forth. She held him until he rolled to the side, bringing her onto his chest.

She made a half-strangled, half-chuckling sound. His arms loosened. "I hurt you?"

She squirmed and contorted on top of him, getting rid of her thong. "No, but that thing surely left a fabric burn on my behind."

He laughed, concentrating on his fingers as they traced her body, enjoying the way her nipples pebbled at his touch. "Sorry."

"You don't sound like it."

He had the strongest urge to pinch her sweet ass, but that would be heaping insult upon injury so he flipped her to her belly to kiss his way down her spine. "Tell me about your tattoos."

She stilled as though surprised by his question. "I got the phoenix when I decided I was going to be a teacher no matter what my parents thought. The 'one life, live it' is pretty self-explanatory."

"But why the film strip?" he asked, running his thumb over the well-done ink.

She hesitated. "It's a reminder that, for better or for worse, our lives are on display. I want to make sure mine inspires—especially for little people."

He blinked, once again surprised by how much he genuinely liked her.

How much he liked how she lived her life.

A knock on the suite door made the hairs rise on the back of his neck.

Something's wrong.

The same feeling he'd had the night the officers had come to tell them his father was dead. The same feeling before his mother's doctor told him about her devastating, incurable disease.

He pushed off from the bed woodenly. Ivy turned over and pulled the sheet up as he reached for his jeans.

"Did you order room service?" When he didn't reply, her smile faded. "What's wrong?"

"Nothing. Stay here." *Where it's safe.* Something heavy backfilled the space where, moments before, he'd felt so free.

He grabbed his phone on the way to the door—why hadn't they knocked again?—and noted that he hadn't missed any calls or texts. He exhaled, then steeled himself as he opened the door.

There was no one there.

Only an envelope with his name written by Shelly's hand.

Don't open it. Three days ago he might not

have, but Ivy had peeled back his layers of cynicism and fear, showing him that he had to meet life with eyes wide open and be ready to take the good with the bad.

He opened the envelope.

If our time together meant anything to you, please meet me at the resort lounge in an hour. I have to tell you something that will forever change your life for the better.

"Who is it?" Ivy asked from his bedroom doorway. She was wrapped in a sheet warmed by their lovemaking, her eyes soft and trusting.

He wouldn't tarnish the moment with Shelly's drama.

He slipped the note in his back pocket and closed the door, guilt and anger and defiance all wrapped up into an ugly knot of unease inside him. "It was nothing."

But even without understanding why, he knew his words were a lie and everything was about to change.

Eleven

Ivy toweled off and slipped into her royal blue, strappy cocktail dress. Grabbing her heels, she sat on her bed, which hadn't been touched since last Friday. Only two more days and she'd have to return to reality. She couldn't wait to see her students again.

But...Cole.

She couldn't let herself think about leaving him yet. The last five days had taken her by surprise. They'd done so much and so little, and all of it so flawless in a messy, completely human sort of way. She felt as real and authentic with Cole as she did with her students.

It was quite unbelievable.

Yesterday, a cold, heavy rain had settled in from the north for an all-day soaker, and they hadn't left their suite once, ordering room service when their appetites had turned to the culinary sort.

They woke in each others' arms this morning with the sun shining on their skin, and it had been a full day of hiking, zip lining, and most recently, paintball.

Cole didn't do anything half way. She loved that and so many other things about him. She'd learned about his family, his colleagues at the fire station who were more family than friends, but the one thing he still wouldn't open up about was Shelly.

When she'd finally mustered the guts to bring it up, he'd shut it down. Something haunted him. Something in his eyes that wasn't there two days ago. Was it from the letter left at their door? He wouldn't talk about it, but he hadn't left her side since he'd received it, so she tried not to worry.

Cole entered their suite with the smile that never failed to make her knees weak. "You look edible."

So did he, even as grubby and paint-splattered as he was. "Did you get a reservation?"

He nodded. "Too bad you've already showered. I could have checked you for ticks." His smirk left no doubt as to how the tick-check would have progressed. He winked at her before stepping into his bathroom and closing the door. Her eyes fell on an envelope sticking out from under his dresser. She bent down to pick it up. It had Cole's name written in a feminine hand. It had to be the one that had upset him two nights ago.

Don't.

How many times had she told her students not to get into someone else's business?

What if it's from Shelly?

After their confrontation with her and Sabrina in the village, Ivy had expected Shelly to disrupt Cole's week every chance she got. But she hadn't. And Ivy and Cole had been inseparable these last few days.

Yet...

Something was happening in the subtext.

As much as Cole tried to hide it, she knew him well enough now—his mannerisms and his body language—to perceive that he was keeping something from her.

She'd grown to like him so much, and

snooping on stuff that wasn't freely shared wasn't the way she operated. She laid the envelope back where she'd found it on the floor. She was walking out of the room when he opened the bathroom door, backlit by the soft glow of the lights and the steam. Her eyes traced the ridged plane of his abs above the low-slung towel he held with one fist.

The cotton towel bulged from his body.

"Come here," he said.

Her knees wobbled slightly as her heels moved soundlessly across the carpet. She wanted to go out and lose herself in the anonymity of the village. If she stayed here in his room, she wouldn't be able to forget about their waning hours. "Why can't I resist you?" she breathed.

He trailed the backs of his fingers down her cheek. "I don't understand it either."

She jumped when someone banged on the door, shouting Cole's name. He reached for his clothes as she ran to the door, heart in her throat.

She pulled the door open to find Shelly's friend Sabrina crying hysterically. She pushed Ivy out of the way, racing across the room to Cole. "She's losing the baby! You have to come, please help her. She's lost so much blood!"

Ivy gripped the back of a dining room chair, stunned into stillness. Cole's face paled. "What the hell are you talking about?"

"Your baby, you fool! She came here to tell you, but you pushed her away at every turn."

He shook his head. "I don't—I'm not— What? *No.*" Then he shut down, his face losing all the openness that had been there moments before.

It was the first fistful of earth tossed on the grave of their brief, fiery romance.

He looked at Ivy, his expression a painful flashback to the first day they'd met. "Ivy..."

Shelly's baby—his baby—was dying. "Go! *Hurry!*" Ivy choked out.

When he dressed and left, she closed the door, barely making it to her bedroom before the first tears in many, many years fell.

Twelve

Cole sat with his head in his hands in the same hospital chair he'd occupied when they'd stuck needles in Ivy. This time he was here for Shelly. He'd had the last hour to think about a baby.

Sixty minutes to wonder how things had gotten so convoluted when he'd aimed for simplicity.

Shelly was sick and alone. When they'd started dating, he'd learned of her bipolar disorder, but he'd never taken the time to think about what that might mean for their future. Or what could happen if she went off her medication. He'd focused on his career and taking care of his family. Shelly was a check mark on his life's to do list. He'd thought they'd marry—not because he couldn't imagine life without her—but because it was the next thing to do in the chronology he'd laid out.

What a damn fool.

He'd thought he was doing the right thing, but he'd only ended up hurting Shelly. He'd ignored her cries for help, just like he'd ignored her note and chosen not to meet her two nights ago.

Absence had been his pattern since the start of their rocky relationship. Shelly might have ultimately broken up with him, but he hadn't ever truly been present.

Ivy had opened his eyes to so much. Being with her never seemed like an obligation. He wanted a life like that—full of passion and seized opportunity—but when it got right down to it, he doubted he could actually overcome his fear of hurting someone he loved by embracing the risks associated with those values.

Cole looked at the clock on the sterile, white wall for the tenth time and began to pace. He would provide for Shelly and the baby, and of course, be a part of the child's life. But could he marry Shelly?

It would be devoid of all the warmth, trust,

and passion such a relationship should be built upon. Empty of all the things he'd experienced with Ivy.

He rubbed his eyes, his chest tight with loss. What could he say to Ivy? They lived in different cities, and their situations, especially his career and his responsibilities to his family, made it tough—if not impossible—to have a long distance relationship after only a week of knowing each other.

Not only that, he couldn't expect her to want to explore what was growing between them when he might soon be father to another woman's child.

Hijo de puta.

"Sir?"

Cole held his breath and looked up at the stern-faced nurse wearing Sesame Street scrubs.

"You can go in now."

* * * *

Ivy wandered in the dawn mist rising from the mountain trail. Eagles soared high in a cloudless sky that promised a gorgeous fall day. Too bad it was her last one to enjoy this magical place.

She trudged onto a narrow boardwalk that led to a cliff overlook. She sank onto the bench and closed bleary eyes. The last time she'd seen Cole was yesterday morning. Felt like eons. He had tried calling and texting multiple times, but she had to get over her selfishness and self-pity. How sick was it that she was feeling resentful of an innocent baby?

Wow, Ivy.

Not her best moment.

She'd slept maybe an hour last night, staying in the village until the last pub had closed. When she'd returned to the castle, she couldn't bear to go back to the suite, and every room in the resort was booked with the jazz festival starting tonight, so she'd wandered through all the wings—settling into a leather chair here, a low, cozy sofa there—sleeping in fits and starts until the restlessness sent her on the move once more.

She had really begun to feel a connection with Cole.

The sex had been spectacular and consuming, but there was more. She knew he felt it, too. He lived and breathed the family values she'd longed for all her life, but never experienced. With someone like Cole— responsible, mature, loyal—she could almost believe in a Hallmark family. Not perfect, but the kind that always pulled together in good

142

times and bad.

With someone like Cole, she'd never feel alone again.

And all those beautiful traits were why he'd never be hers. Because if Shelly's baby survived, he'd stand by her because it was the right thing to do.

She was definitely falling for him. Would have loved the opportunity to see where this went.

Stop feeling sorry for yourself.

She stood up from the bench and stepped to the guardrail. It was a long, scary way down. Her belly fluttered and her hands tightened on the safety rail, but she didn't feel as lightheaded as she would have only a week earlier. At least she'd be able to tell her kids that she'd taken strides toward overcoming her fear of heights.

She was about to pull out her camera when activity attracted her attention fifty yards to the left on a long foot bridge that connected two rocky outcroppings. Someone staggered onto the bridge from the opposite side. A gust of wind from the gorge below blew the woman's coat hood back.

Blonde hair. *Shelly?*

Ivy's pulse kicked up. She speed-walked to the bridge, breaking into a jog when Cole came running from the opposite side of the bridge where Shelly had emerged moments earlier.

What was going on?

Shelly stopped in the middle of the bridge, looking down at the rocks and foliage some twenty yards below the swaying structure. More wind stole up from the gorge, lifting her snarly hair so that it floated in eerie weightlessness.

Nearing the edge of the bridge from her side, Ivy could hear Shelly shout at Cole, her back to Ivy. "Don't come any closer! I'm warning you."

Cole complied, halting at the mouth of the bridge. Ivy's gaze sought his across the chasm, her heart clawing up her throat. His face was grim, his lips pulled into a straight line, his olive complexion sallow, like he was coming off a long convalescence.

"Come on, Shelly. We can walk while you rage at me on the trails," he called, his movements now almost imperceptible. So slow and controlled that Shelly wasn't even aware he was inching onto the bridge.

"If I jump, you wouldn't care!"

Oh, Lord, no. What had happened between these two in the last twenty hours? Was the baby okay? What should she do?

"If I didn't care about you, I wouldn't be here." Cole's voice floated across the chasm, making Ivy's heart ache for Shelly. Losing Cole would leave an overwhelming hole because now she knew what she'd be missing.

The cable bridge swayed under Shelly's jolting movements as she followed Cole's gaze to Ivy on the opposite bank. She cried out like a wounded animal, crumbling to the wood planks. "Go away, you've ruined my life! Don't you see how you've come between us?"

"I'm so sorry for your pain, Shelly." The words scraped Ivy's throat. The bridge appeared well-built, but it groaned and shivered, and Jesus, would it hold under all this activity? Growing pressure in Ivy's chest made it hard to draw a full breath. Panic quivered at the edges of her consciousness. *Don't look down.* Her gaze skittered back to Cole. Everything about his body language communicated control, his composure easing some of her anxiety.

He was calm in the storm. Placid in the face of emergencies.

Help him help Shelly.

145

He broke their stare, took two slow steps, and extended a hand to his ex.

Shelly spun to face him. "Leave me alone, both of you!"

Her voice was so desperate, her suffering so poignant, Ivy's hands clasped in front of her heart. She stepped tentatively onto the bridge, counting to ten and back again to keep her mind busy. *Ohmygodohmygod. Don't look down.*

"If you take one more step, I swear I'll jump."

Cole and Ivy froze.

Cole was six feet away from Shelly. "I wasn't there when you needed me. I'll always regret that. But this time, I promise I'll help you find resources to get well."

On her knees, Shelly slammed her fists on the wood planks again and again, bloodying them, rocking the bridge as she screamed. "I'm not sick. I'm sad! Nothing works out for me. I *lose*. Every time."

Ivy's hands curled around the cable railing for balance. Shelly squeezed through the safety cables between the hand rails, fingers clasped above her head as though she was about to dive to the rocky floor below.

"No!" Ivy and Cole lunged at the same time. Cole wrapped his arm around Shelly's shins. Ivy managed to grab hold of her left arm. The downward inertia of Shelly's falling body slammed Ivy and Cole into the metal cables. Ivy's heart hammered so hard she felt dizzy. She dropped to her belly on the planks to center her gravity and stop her slide over the edge. Sweat stung her eyes and made her grip slick against Shelly's skin.

Cole grunted and swore, wedging his feet between the floor boards for leverage. Shelly kicked and screamed, and hot fury swarmed inside Ivy. "Goddamn it, stop fighting or you're going to kill us and the baby, too!" she cried.

All the fight went out of Shelly. Her body went limp as a huge sob tore from her throat. Ivy's arms, shoulders, and abs screamed from the effort of hanging on, even though Cole had most of Shelly's weight.

Now that Shelly wasn't fighting, Cole hauled her back onto the bridge in moments. He only allowed them a couple of deep breaths before he picked her up and carried her off the bridge back the way he'd come.

Ivy followed a little ways behind on jello-legs, gulping huge lungs full of air. Cole set

Shelly gently down on a sunlit patch of grass, speaking softly. Ivy closed her eyes because it actually hurt to look at him, knowing he could never be hers.

She shivered, her eyes snapping open when his fingers ran down her cheek. She would feel his phantom touch for a long time to come.

"Thank you for helping," he said.

She tried to smile. "I hope she'll be okay."

His eyes burned hot. "Ivy...she faked the pregnancy. Stole a fucking blood bag from the clinic and pretended she was miscarrying," he whispered emphatically. "You and I need to talk, but I need to get her some help first. Will you wait for me at the suite?"

Ivy stared blankly, trying to assimilate everything he'd said.

"Ivy?"

"Okay."

Cole's fingers squeezed her shoulders, making her throat tighten. "Good. That's real good." His smile was a cool drink of water after an endless sojourn through the Sahara.

Then he turned back to Shelly, helped her to her feet, and supported her as they made their way down the trail back to the resort. When they vanished behind the first stand of trees, Cole didn't bother to look back. The relentless desert returned to Ivy's heart. This wasn't over yet.

Not even remotely.

Thirteen

Ivy started, glancing up from the stack of papers she was supposed to be grading, when a flock of students rushed to the windows, chattering animatedly and pointing at something below the classroom's second story perch. Her lips curved into a tired smile. She had never been more grateful for her fourth graders' energy than when she returned to Grand Junction without having said goodbye to Cole.

He'd never returned to their suite.

She'd waited all day and into the night for him. No calls. Not even a text.

She finally rented a car and checked out of the resort at three am, unable to sleep.

Unable to even cry.

Then yesterday morning, when she'd

returned to class, these sweet little faces had triggered her tears for several embarrassing moments. She'd told them it was one of the best trips of her life. But sometimes even the good times made her sad when they came to an end.

Bittersweet became their word of the week.

She gave them the silver lining—she'd faced her fear of heights—but she was left with so many questions. She could have reached out to Cole, but since he'd never shown up after he asked her to wait for him, the ball was in his court.

If he didn't pick it up, well, she wouldn't be *that* girl.

It hurt that he didn't think enough of her to be honest and tell her he'd changed his mind. She'd been so sure—had felt it right down in her bones—that he was as crazy about her as she was about him.

It would be a while before she'd trust her instincts again.

She sighed and stood up, grateful for the diversion at the window, because she was too weary to grade papers anyway. It was a warm, sunny day. Maybe there was a way to incorporate their last lesson of the day outdoors.

She made her way to the students swarming by the window, the words *fire trucks* and *firemen* penetrating her musings. Her heart stalled, then restarted with a kick in her chest.

"What are they doing with that ladder, Ms. Ivy?"

Fire trucks. Three of them by the curb in front of the school. And firemen, probably a dozen milling around, smiling as a man in a yellow helmet put his foot on the first rung of the truck's ladder, his navy blue tee shirt stretched tightly across broad shoulders.

A *Poudre Fire Authority* shirt.

Meaning Fort Collins.

Oh my God.

"He's climbing up to *our* room!" a girl in pig tails screamed ecstatically, igniting an explosive fourth grade cacophony.

Their excited voices faded as Ivy braced her hand against the window frame, trying to process what was happening. Half way up the ladder, Cole looked up from under the helmet's brim, his lips curving in a dashing smile that made her heart pound so hard she felt faint.

One of the larger boys managed to open one of the double-hung windows, leaving only the screen between Cole and her classroom. Ivy couldn't take her eyes off him as he greeted the kids, then winked and put a finger to his lips, silencing them so fast it could have been a magic spell.

What did the shadows beneath his eyes mean? She ached to pull him to her, to lay him down and hold him close so he could rest long and deep. His gaze warmed her for a moment before he addressed the students.

"Did you know you have the best teacher in the whole world?"

A chorus of *yessss!* was followed by a small voice, "Are you Ms. Ivy's bittersweet?"

Oh, damn. They were so intuitive.

Cole looked at Ivy, a gamut of emotions chasing across his strong features before he turned back to his mini inquisitor. "If I am, little chief, I'm not leaving until I fix it."

A lump settled in Ivy's throat. Chatter flowed behind her as more students filed into the room. She almost jumped out of her skin when Kay and Monique drew up beside her like a phalanx.

"I knew he'd make some grand gesture if he was as extraordinary as you made him out to be," Kay said.

Monique hummed deep in her throat. "*Mmm-mmm-mmm*, would you look at that bangin' body? Lord have mercy!"

Ivy didn't trust herself to speak. A boy in a Broncos' jersey pressed his nose into the glass beside the open window. "Why are you on a ladder?" he yelled, fogging up the glass.

Cole's warm hazel eyes caressed Ivy. "Did she tell you she's not afraid of heights anymore?"

The students cheered.

Crap, no no no. "Cole."

This time he smiled with teeth.

"The superintendent said I could take the screen off as long as no children were present, and I didn't use my hatchet," he said, and he proceeded to do just that. The principal and school counselor helped Kay and Monique usher the students out of the room and outside where they'd spend the final thirty minutes of the school day climbing aboard the red and white trucks and trying on bulky fireman's garb.

When Ivy turned back to Cole, he was leaning into the room, setting the screen on the floor as if entering school from a second story window was a perfectly normal thing to do on a Friday afternoon. Her pulse beat furiously in her neck. "What are you doing, Cole?"

* * * *

The wariness in Ivy's expression warred with her natural sense of adventure that had so captivated him from the beginning. He didn't blame her for being guarded, especially since he hadn't communicated at all after the bridge incident. "I'm taking a risk. I don't want regrets when it comes to you."

"Why didn't you come back, or at least call or text?"

"I'm sorry. I should have, but things got crazy, and I didn't know how to say everything over the phone. Ivy, it was insane. Shelly swallowed half a bottle of pills while I was on the phone with a doctor. An hour later, Mya called to say our mother was in the emergency room with breathing problems. She made it through the night, but the doctor told us it was time to make alternate living arrangements for her."

"Oh, Cole. How is she now? And Shelly?"

"Mom's settled and okay. More okay with the situation than I am. Shelly's in the hospital.

They're working on getting her the right mix of meds."

Ivy nodded, then backed away from the window. "Come in, I don't want you falling off that ladder onto one of the kids," she scolded.

He let her help him into the room just so he could touch her. When she released his hand, it was all he could do not to scoop her up and force her to admit she'd missed him as much as he missed her. He took off his helmet and set it on her desk. "After moving mom, I caught up with my siblings, paid the bills, grabbed a couple hours of sleep, then went to work for my twenty four hour shift. I got off at seven-thirty this morning and jumped in my truck. A buddy of mine has a brother who works in one of the stations here in Grand Junction. He called in a couple of favors to get this spectacle approved for me." He took her hands, kissed her knuckles, then rubbed them against the stubble on his cheek. Children's laughter floated up from the fire trucks parked at the curb. "Ivy, I was never ready to let this go. I had to take care of my family, but I couldn't wait to get here to see you. I'll deal with being the butt of two city fire departments' jokes for another chance to be with you."

Her eyes welled as she smiled, a soft curve of her lips that made him weak and invincible all at once.

"This is terribly gallant, Mr. Castillo. And creative."

"But is it working?" He held his breath.

She edged closer. That lime and coconut scent that was so much a part of her was like a welcome home. Her nails scraped along the nape of his neck. "You should know by now I like the road less traveled."

So true. And one of the many reasons he was falling so hard for her. He leaned down and feathered his lips—soft as breath—against hers. "Our week together changed my life. Some people make the world look completely different. Make it finally look *right*. People who make you want to be the best version of yourself. Does that sound stupid?" She shook her head, her beautiful blue eyes shimmering with unshed tears. "You're that person to me, Ivy. I don't know how to do this next part where we go back to our separate lives, but the thought of not trying to hold things together is unacceptable. Tell me you want to see where this goes."

He'd beg if he had to.

157

* * * *

His eyes demanded her agreement. She'd never let him beg, but because she couldn't talk right now without bleating like a lost lamb, she nodded and leaned into him.

"*Ivy*." Such a sexy groan. His warm lips claimed hers while his arms wrapped around her like she was a treasure. His thumbs slipped beneath the hem of her shirt, stroking her skin, fueling her passion like he always did.

She laid a hand over his steady heartbeat, took a deep breath, and dove. "I don't let people in. It's easier—*safer*—to keep them entertained at arm's length. I only let myself be vulnerable in ways that don't have consequences. The real me—the one who's always wanted someone to put me first—hides behind smiles and pleasantries. I've always known that about myself, but I never asked why. The way you live your life—so honest and with so much integrity—pushed me to evaluate things I've ignored for a long time. It's easier *not* to, you know?"

"I do," he said, and she *knew* he did. Everything he'd told her regarding his guilt about Stan's death, his remorse over fighting with his father before his murder...

Yeah, Cole knew all about collateral damage when you didn't confront your demons.

And he understood the devastating loneliness you could create when all you really wanted was connection.

"With you, I couldn't keep the barrier up if I wanted to. And the strangest thing is, I don't *want* to. Instead I need you to know everything about me because if you don't, it would never work. I get that now. You're the first person who has ever made me want to take that chance. The first person who makes me feel free and safe."

He squeezed her tightly to his chest. "Maybe it's because you puked on our first date, and I didn't run?" His voice rumbled against her cheek.

She laughed and threaded her hands through his hair once more. "There are definite perks to dating a fireman, I guess. Your cast iron stomach in the face of messy realities is one of them. Good thing, too, because I can't cook for crap."

"It's definitely your lucky day then because I'm one of the best cooks in our station. I hope you like spice, though, because I bring some heat."

No. Joke.

His wandering hands slid down her back to cup her bottom, bringing her flush with the oh-so-perfect fit of his jeans.

"I like flirting with fire, especially when I know you've got my back."

"You know I do," he breathed against her mouth.

"What happens tomorrow?" She looked down to where her fingers rested against his chest.

"Hey." He brought her chin up so she would look at him. "Obstacles are those scary things you see when you take your eyes off the goal. I've faced lots of them. I could give you all kinds of corny clichés here, but if we want this bad enough, we'll find a way. We're less than five hours apart, and I'm on a twenty-four hours on, forty-eight hours off schedule. I'll drive to Grand Junction as often as I can, provided Mya can help out with our siblings. It won't be easy, but the best things never are."

She pulled him down for a long, deep kiss that had them both breathing heavy by the time they came up for air. "I want to meet your family," she blurted.

His eyes softened, his thumbs tracing her lips. "I want to show you off in my home town more than anything."

Her heart skipped a beat at the earnestness in his voice.

Fort Collins had a great school system from what she'd heard.

But that discussion could come another day.

She glanced at the ladder in the open window, trying not to let her old fears resurface. "I suppose I should get this over with, huh?"

Five minutes later, amid fanfare from the students and adults gathered below, they descended the ladder. Half an hour after that, she had her fireman right where she wanted him. She pushed him onto her bed and straddled his powerful hips. "Now, about that heat you've been bragging about..."

His lips curved nice and slow and terribly tempting. "Yeah, you want some of that, *mi reina*?"

Oh, God, yes, please. She stripped off the shirt that was suddenly way too damn confining.

"I'll take that as a yes," he laughed, and she was too far gone to feel any shame.

Besides, this was her Cole.

She didn't need to hide anything from him. He saw all, knew all, and accepted her anyway.

When their clothes were in haphazard piles on the floor, the bed, and the lampshade, her fireman brought the heat.

She burned, and then he quenched.

And it was the perfect seal on the promise he'd made for their tomorrow.

Misty would love for you to check out the other Noble Pass Affaire titles by Chick Swagger. Here's a sneak peek at *Flirting with Disaster* by Josie Matthews...

Flirting with Disaster
A Noble Pass Affaire Novella

"Beckette. My name is Beckette." He lifted her ankle onto his lap and removed her shoe. He ran his hand over the small amount of swelling that had started. "I'm sorry I hurt you. I'm a bastard and tend to hurt people when they get close. It's my curse. That's why I avoid emotional attachments." He smirked. "As if I were even capable."

Like finding two almonds in a bite size Almond Joy, her future flashed brightly in her mind. Yes, he'd be *the one*.

Her heart beat wildly as she reviewed the ramifications of what she wanted to do...seduce him. Seduce Beckette, The Beast, the man of mystery and beauty. She wanted this emotionally stunted, beautiful man to be the one to take her virginity, move her to the next level of her life.

Father her child…without him knowing, of course. She didn't need a man. Not that he'd want her or she'd ever want him. He was a perfect stranger never to be thought of again.

She was ovulating. She'd always had her menses schedule plotted in her brain. Now all she had to do was get him to take her to bed.

It was ludicrous. It was unethical. But she was desperate.

Our little bundle of joy will be arriving in May!

She pulled her foot from Count Drac's lap then stood and slid off her other shoe. She paced the small room without a limp. Her nerves had numbed the pain. He watched her, humor lighting his secretive eyes. This man was dangerous, hardened, disreputable. Perfect for an unscrupulous mission.

But he was also smart. She needed to include that in her calculations.

"I'm fine, really." She stood with her back to him and covertly unbuttoned the top of her blouse. Cleavage. Men liked cleavage. She turned and tried to swing her hair in the sultry way women did. Her head thudded against a gourd lantern hanging from a shelf.

Smooth.

He leaned back on his hands and smirked, his eyes zeroing in on her burgeoning breasts. She had a good bosom, she'd been told. It'd be advantageous to use her positive attributes to the best of her ability.

She noted his body language—visual interest, pulsating carotid in the neck, relaxed posture, erection.

All promising signs.

* * * *

Beck almost came in his jeans right then and there. "Yes, you are."

What was this naive, little, tabby cat up to? Parading around his fucking bedroom like some vixen in heat.

She placed her hand just above that magnificent rack and took a deep breath. "Okay, how do we do this? Do we just start? Do I pay you first?"

He practically choked. Was she serious? Beck examined her flawless face. Yeah, she was serious...and nervous as hell. This might actually be fun, to a point. "Depends on what you're looking for, Sweetheart." He held back a smirk.

165

Jude paced back and forth in front of him, driving him nuts with the wiggle in her hips. "Sex. I'd like to have sex with you." She faced him, her eyes wide and pleading, then held her palm in the air, facing him. "Nothing crazy. Just plain missionary would be acceptable. Do you have a current health history on hand?" Her little ass twitched as she rushed to her huge backpack and dumped it on his bed. The woman had everything in there to survive quite nicely on a deserted island. She grabbed a banded file the size of an envelope then whipped out a piece of paper. She held it toward him in her trembling hand. "Here's mine. I always carry it with me for emergencies. I'm free of all STDs."

Beck just stared. The woman was certifiable.

And fucking innocently sexy as all hell.

He didn't do innocent, but this game was an amusing distraction from his own frustrations. He leaned forward and rested his elbows on his knees as she waited for a response, standing there holding out that damn health history.

"Do you like to be tied up, Jude?" he whispered.

Her eyes widened.

"Because I charge more for bondage and

threesomes are definitely out. I only work one-on-one. If you'd like to incorporate sex toys it will be an extra fifty a night. Seventy-five if I have to provide batteries."

The paper drifted from her stiff hands and floated to the floor at his feet. Her sensuous lips parted. Her quick intake of her breath and the way her breasts rose did nothing to calm his libido. He almost felt guilty for toying with her.

She didn't respond so he tweaked a little harder, relishing this small window of joy to brighten his dark existence. "Now, role-playing is a whole other price list. Depending on the role and the cost of the costumes and props, it could run you into the thousands. I do a great dominating circus clown." He pulled his T-shirt over his head.

She hesitantly reached out, ran one soft hand down the center of his chest, exploring him in a slow descent, making every nerve in his body burn with a yearning and desire he'd never felt.

The witch's touch blew his mind.

Sex had always been just a physical release with him. A way to forget the pain.

But this was…different.

He inhaled sharply as her little hands

167

mapped his form. It was as if she'd never seen a half-naked man before. Christ, she'd almost been married. She had to have seen at least one.

"Can you do a Russian accent with that circus clown? Can we turn out the lights?"

Beck slowly shook his head. "*Nyet.* I need to see where I'm going."

Her mouth formed an 'O' as she continued her visual consumption of his body. She stepped back and fastidiously undid each button on her shirt, keeping her eyes on the job. Once she'd exposed all that beautiful skin sprinkled with golden freckles and the pink, lacy bra lovingly holding those gorgeous breasts, she lifted her eyes to his. "Okay, let's proceed. Do you need a deposit up front? Where do you want me to lie down?"

Jesus H. Christ. She was going to be the death of him. And it irked him that she acted like she was being asked to clean his toilet. But Miss Duffy was always tense and, God help him, he couldn't stop himself from reaching out to stroke the velvet skin on her shoulder. Couldn't refrain from touching his lips to her pale skin for a small taste. He was fascinated by this shy, nervous version of her. She was like a drug to him, calling out, luring him in, placing a spell on him.

He bent his head and kissed the side of her neck. Soft, silky, and the smell... He couldn't get enough. Clean, fresh and spicy. Like lavender. The same scent he'd noticed in her room.

He was done.

And now, a sneak peek from Misty's book, *COME HELL OR HIGH DESIRE*, available October 2015 at Amazon and Barnes & Noble:

Come Hell or High Desire

Sloane's fingernails suddenly raked at her skull.

"Lord! I almost forgot. We *have* to go back to Ann's. She has a diary!"

Zack swerved into an empty parking lot and swiveled to face her, blood pounding in his ears. "What are you talking about?"

"Ann keeps a diary. We have to find it."

"You're just telling me this *now?* You should have goddamn said something right away!"

"Don't you dare curse at me like that, you seismic jackass!"

He had to get *out*. He flung the truck door open and strode onto the cracked asphalt. Her door slammed shut moments later, and within seconds she was wagging a finger in his face.

"And don't you walk away from me, either!"

"Then don't be such a damn shrew."

Color flooded over her cheekbones seconds before she punched him in the gut. Hard. An ancient fire lit up his nerve circuits and adrenaline had him widening his stance. His heart gunned. His groin tightened.

And she was still shrill.

"I'm *not* a shrew! How am I supposed to act in a situation like this? You think I'm enjoying this? I *hate* it! But unfortunately I have a conscience which would haunt me for the rest of my life if I don't follow this through until we have some answers. You came to me and wanted to rule out the church first. Then with everything that happened, I forgot about the diary until right now. That clear enough for you, you—"

Clear enough, honey.

He vised her head between his palms and kissed her. He hadn't meant to, but the moment her mouth opened to his, he was lost. Not breaking contact with her mouth, he wrapped one arm around her, his hand splaying across her ass, locking her hips against him. Her hands were in his hair, her hips grinding, driving him crazy. They feasted on each other's mouth, tongues dueling, daring, seeking. He felt her fingers between their bodies, slipping underneath the waistband of his jeans, pulling at the hem of his shirt. Her fingernail scraped his abs and he groaned. She leaned away from his mouth, her eyes dead sexy. Liquid brown. He was gonna—

A car horn blew, jerking him back to life. Back to the parking lot. He looked over to see a man in a black minivan at a stoplight giving them the thumbs up. He honked twice more, waved, and drove on.

Sloane burst into a fit of laughter that quickly dissolved into tears.

That clinched it. He'd woken up this morning in some creepy-assed Twilight Zone.

He wiped away her tears and laid his forehead against hers for a few moments to get his brain rewired. Then he guided her over to the passenger side of the truck, opened the door, and nudged her inside. He walked around to the driver's side, then eased into the seat, adjusting this way and that to accommodate the monster in his jeans.

Sloane sniffed loudly. "Now can we go to Ann's?"

He banged his head against the steering wheel before glancing at her profile. Her fingers fidgeted in her lap.

Looks. Brains. Compassion. Sense of humor.

Add to that one heaping dose of courage and what do you get?

Zack totally FUBAR.

Definitely time to cut her loose. "What if we're dealing with some psycho here? Doesn't that scare you?" That dimmed the light in those hellcat eyes.

"Well...yeah. But it's too late for me to back out now. Besides, who do you trust with my safety more...you or the police who don't even know there might be foul play yet?"

Nailed. The woman already knew how to manipulate him. He gave her the scowl he saved for employees who were caught dicking around. "You're really a piece of work." He'd hoped to tick her off, but she actually *smiled* at him. He rubbed his cheek to stop himself from smiling back. "Okay. But before we go to Ann's, you're going to tell me why I feel like I'm hooked up to a navy submarine generator every time I touch you."

Her smile slipped. She shifted on the leather seat, brushing some imaginary lint off her blouse. *Aha.* He *knew* there was something to it.

Seconds ticked by. He purposely turned down the A/C. Then, keeping his eyes between her and the rearview mirror, he laid his right hand on the top of her seat again, only this time his thumb brushed the bare skin of her neck. Pulses of energy jumped under his skin.

Her gaze flew to his.

Busted, little woman.

"You play mean."

"Not mean, Goldie. *Equal.*"

A few more seconds of silence ticked by while sweat gathered a bead to run between his pecs. He leaned his head back against the seat and narrowed his eyes to slits so he could still use his peripheral vision to keep tabs on her and any activity outside the truck. She brought a hand up to inspect her nails. Then rummaged through her purse until she came out with a nail file, which she promptly tossed on the dash before reaching over to flip the A/C on high.

"Fine! Along with the visions, I sometimes have the ability to be attuned to the energy of others."

Zack studied her, feeling a curious lightness in his chest. She fixed her hat on her head like it was a piece of body armor.

"I don't know why it's so strong with you. Nor why your energy doesn't suck the life out of me like most other people's does if it sneaks past my barriers." She was inspecting her nails again. He brushed the backs of his fingers along her jawbone and felt her shiver.

She looked at him with such naked vulnerability it robbed his breath. "And the fact that you also feel this connection is totally unbelievable. It's...I don't share that part of myself with anyone. If I even tried to explain what happens to me... Lord, people would think I was a freak. *Know* I'm a freak."

That she should have to hide parts of herself from the world caused anger to surge through him. His fingers trailed along the exposed column of her neck. "I've met a lot of freaks over the years, and trust me, you don't qualify."

About the Author
Misty Dietz

Misty's love affair with words started in middle school with moody stories set in exotic locales she knew nothing about. In college, her boy-angst erupted in disturbing reams of poetry. After grad school, the writing went into hibernation until she found her own happily-ever-after with an ultra linear man who is the long-suffering counter-balance to her zig-zagging ways. Now, she spends her days writing sexy, adrenaline-fueled stories, enjoying family and friends, and praying her children don't come home with math homework.

Find her online at www.MistyDietz.com, or if you're a social media addict like her, stop by her Facebook page or say hey on Twitter @MistyDietz.

www.Facebook.com/MistyDietzWriter

www.Twitter.com/MistyDietz

Made in the USA
Middletown, DE
29 July 2015